LUCIA HAD LOST THE ONE THING SHE HAD NOT IMAGINED LOSING—HER HEART

When Lucia entered the household of Hugo, Marquis of Mandersely, she was prepared for any threat to her honor that the notorious nobleman might pose to her.

What Lucia was not prepared for was her reaction when Hugo calmly ignored her as he fell prey to the sophisticated charms of the beautiful Countess de Treves.

What Lucia never suspected was that her greatest danger might come from the blackmailing schemes and lustful designs of the elegant and evil Sir Gideon Benedict.

What Lucia never dreamed of was the labyrinth of intrigue, adventure, abduction, and suspense that awaited her as she played a desperate game to thwart the man she hated, and to overcome all odds in winning the infuriating and irresistible man she loved.

Big Bestsellers from SIGNET

The GOLDEN SONGBIRD

by
Sheila F. Walsh

A SIGNET BOOK
NEW AMERICAN LIBRARY
TIMES MIRROR

Published by arrangement with Hurst & Blackett Ltd.

SIGNET TRADEMARK REG. U.S. PAT. OFF. AND FOREIGN COUNTRIES
REGISTERED TRADEMARK—MARCA REGISTRADA
HECHO EN CHICAGO, U.S.A.

SIGNET, SIGNET CLASSICS, MENTOR, PLUME AND MERIDIAN BOOKS
are published by The New American Library, Inc.,
1301 Avenue of the Americas, New York, New York 10019

FIRST PRINTING, JULY, 1975

4 5 6 7 8 9

If you build a nest in your heart,
the singing bird will come.
—Chinese proverb

◆ Chapter *1* ◆

In the heavily curtained little salon, a solitary pendant lamp spilled light onto the baize-covered table near the window, making it a brilliant focal point in a well of shadows.

If there was tension in the air, Hugo, fourth Marquis of Mandersely, seemed unaware of it. He sprawled in his chair with all the indolent ease of one born to command—the complete man of fashion, from his dark hair, styled à la Titus, to the long legs stretched out before him, encased in pale yellow skin-tight pantaloons. An exquisitely cut coat of dark blue superfine was thrown carelessly open, to reveal a half-buttoned waistcoat of richly striped white satin.

His chin was sunk deep in the intricate folds of his cravat, and the pale, saturnine features wore an expression of acute boredom. Between long, slim fingers an empty wineglass rotated gently.

Toby Blanchard knew that expression of old, and sighed. The evening had been a sad mistake from the outset and would undoubtedly earn him one of Hugo's stinging set-downs.

For it was he who had first become acquainted with their host, Mr. Jasper Franklyn, some days earlier. He had been with old Lord Brancaster, who, though known to be a trifle touched in the upper works, was still alert enough to spot a wrong 'un, or so Toby had thought. When Mr. Franklyn had learned that the Marquis of Mandersely, that noted young man, was none other than Toby's cousin, he had at once insisted that he should bring him around to Bruton Street one evening for a hand of cards, and Toby, being an amiable, easygoing young man, had agreed readily enough.

Glancing now at their host, slumped untidily across the table, an unfashionable rumpled wig masking his balding head and his face an unhealthy shade of purple as he fixed Hugo with an unwavering stare, Toby was forced to admit that he had been sadly taken in. Mr. Franklyn had spent the best part of the evening trying to outdrink Hugo, and his fine manners had degenerated inevitably into coarseness.

A log stirred in the grate and settled, sending up a shower of sparks.

Lord Mandersely raised his head and set the glass upon the table. "Well gentlemen?" he drawled. "Are we all agreed to call it a night?"

Mr. Franklyn glared resentfully at the pile of gold and slips of paper casually heaped in front of his lordship—much of it Mr. Franklyn's own money. He was a reckless gambler, but a poor loser. Moreover, he could not bear the thought of all that money leaving his house in the pockets of one already overendowed with worldly goods.

Things were not working out at all as Mr. Franklyn had envisioned. He was a man of almost fanatical single-mindedness, a quality that had enabled him to amass a considerable fortune from his ever-growing chain of mills in north Yorkshire. In his fiftieth year, he had decided to take a house in London and live in a manner befitting a man of his wealth and stature. To this end he had married a beautiful and much traveled foreign lady, a widow, who had intimated that she could smooth his path into Society. But she had proved a bitter disappointment, succumbing to a fever within a very short space of time and leaving him with the encumbrance of a young stepdaughter who despised him as much as he disliked her.

He had made some progress, however. That old fool Brancaster had put him up for one or two of the better clubs. He had even acquired a thin veneer of culture, and with a steadily mounting fortune he was convinced that all he needed was a stroke of luck. Meeting Captain Blanchard had seemed just that; this cousin of his was everything that Franklyn most envied and desired to emulate.

But the evening had proved a trying one from the start. He had discovered his lordship to be damnably top-lofty, and in an effort to puff himself up he had resorted too often to the port bottle, to the detriment of both his character and his judgment. His play grew even wilder and more ill-judged as it became apparent that the marquis was enjoying a phenomenal run of luck. By now he was in no condition to think straight.

"You can't leave yet, my lord," he grumbled.

"Why, it's scarcely past eleven o' the clock! You must give us a chance to win back some of our money."

Mandersely raised a languid hand to stifle a yawn.

Toby eyed him nervously; any minute now he was going to be devilish unpleasant! He said hurriedly, "Not I, Franklyn! My pockets are all to let!"

The fourth member of the party, an insignificant little man named Thane, who, like Toby, piped up in thin, reedy tones that he also found the play quite above his touch.

Enraged, Franklyn slapped a dice box on the table. "Right, then, Mandersely—whatever's there, I'll double it ... throw you for the lot! One throw apiece, highest wins!"

There was a gasp of disapproval from Thane. Toby stared, incredulous.

The marquis merely raised one eyebrow a fraction. "You *do* realize how much is here, my friend?" he murmured softly.

"I should; most of it's mine!"

"And are you really prepared to cover it?"

Franklyn began to curse. Toby cut in with forced joviality, "Best call it a night, my dear fellow; we're all a bit the worse for wear, and Hugo's had the devil's luck all evening! Can't hope to overturn it at a stroke."

"Keep out of this, Blanchard! I don't need any pretty soldier boy to hold my hand! I ain't got so much money in the house, Mandersely," he blustered, "but I can cover that amount ten times over. You'll take a note?"

Lord Mandersely sighed. "I think not. I already

10

appear to have a considerable number of your IOU's. Some other time, perhaps?"

The insult was so thinly veiled that Toby held his breath. Franklyn pulled himself unsteadily to his feet, his face livid. Out in the hall a door closed. A look of cunning flickered for a moment in his eyes. "Wait!" he muttered thickly. His lurching progress across the room was hampered by a chair, which he kicked and flung aside.

"My dear Toby," drawled his lordship, refilling his glass and leaning back to regard the glowing liquid through narrowed eyes. "Army life is ruining your powers of discrimination! If this is how you are now choosing your friends, I shall be forced to deny myself the pleasure of your company."

Mr. Thane glared and Toby, incensed by this slur upon the Ninety-fifth Rifles, opened his mouth to utter a stinging retort, and paused. Hugo had that devilish glitter about the eyes, and no one but a congenital idiot would risk provoking Mandersely when he'd broached his third bottle. So he only muttered, "Do be quiet, Hugo! If you want to give me a trimming, do it later. He'll hear you!"

"I wish he might, dear boy. In fact, I wish profoundly that I had obeyed my earlier instincts and refused the invitation. The fellow's a damned Cit!"

A high complaining voice cut in. "Lord Mandersely! It ill-becomes you, I think, to speak so of one who is your host."

My lord lifted cool eyes to regard Mr. Edwin Thane. He raised his eye glass and allowed it to travel very slowly over that gentleman's person. It took in the puce satin coat, which so ill-became his sallow skin, and lingered for a long, unbelieving moment over the cravat. Under this silent scrutiny Mr. Thane quickly turned the same color as his offending garment. Satisfied at last, the marquis turned back to Toby.

"What the devil is the fellow about now?"

Franklyn had flung open the door and was bellowing like a bull. "Lucia ... is that you, girl? Come here, damn you!"

Toby frowned. "That's the stepdaughter, ain't it? The one we met earlier?"

His cousin smiled thinly, recalling the knowing way Franklyn had led her forward to be presented to him as "my little Lucia."

There was nothing *jeune fille* about the vivid emerald gown cut too low across the bosom and clinging to every slim, seductive curve. True, she was uncommon enough to warrant a second glance, though blondes were not generally to his taste. It was an interesting face, delicately formed, dominated by luminous green eyes fringed with dark lashes and dark, finely arched brows which flicked up at the outer corners to lend a certain elfin charm. Her hair was of a pale gold, unusually shaded and dressed elaborately high.

The girl's function was so obvious that he almost laughed aloud. They should have known that he had been pursued by far cleverer women than this chit of a girl who had lifted her chin so imperiously when he put up his glass to inspect her. At the age of thirty-one he was too much a veteran to succumb to so blatant an attempt to cast out lures.

A heated argument appeared to be in progress in the hallway; a low, agonized whisper filtered in through the open doorway.

"Sir, I cannot! I have retired for the night! I merely slipped down to the library for a book."

There was a bellow of rage.

"Don't stand there arguing with me, my wench! You know what that'll get you! You'll do as I bid you!" Mr. Franklyn lurched back into the room, half-dragging the girl. She was clad only in a dressing robe, which she was desperately trying to clutch around her.

Franklyn pushed her roughly toward the lighted table and slumped back into his chair.

"Now, my lord. Since my signature don't please you, I will offer you a more tempting wager. My stepdaughter against your winnings!"

There was a sharp cry from the girl, followed by a stunned silence. Toby's chair crashed backward. "It's monstrous! You can't do it, man!"

Thane rose also, adding his own querulous objections.

The marquis alone appeared unmoved. Only his eyes widened a little, watching the girl's reactions. A brilliant flush had died away, leaving her deathly pale. She made an instinctive movement to draw her robe more closely about her slim figure, and stood very straight and with remarkable composure as his eyes slowly raked her from head to bare pink feet.

She looked much younger and very vulnerable with her lovely hair brushed straight and loose about her face. The eyes were enormous dark pools, but they stared back at him with defiance. Only the rapid rise and fall of her bosom betrayed her.

Egad! You're a cool one, thought Hugo with a flicker of admiration.

Toby was addressing himself to the girl. "Beg you, Miss Mannering ... *do* retire ... all a ghastly misunderstanding ... should never have happened...." He swung around. "Hugo, tell the man you'll have no part of this nonsense!"

The marquis was about to do so when the girl spoke in a low clear voice with just a suspicion of a tremor. "It is good of you to show so much concern on my behalf, Captain Blanchard, but there is no misunderstanding. My stepfather has proposed a wager. Does his lordship wish to accept it or not?"

There was an unmistakable challenge in the words, and even more in the look that accompanied them. Right, my fine miss! thought Hugo. If that's the way you want to play it. It's a sharp lesson you're needing!

He took from his pocket a fine enameled snuffbox. Without taking his eyes from the girl, he flicked it open, and with a delicate turn of the wrist he took a pinch, inhaled, and snapped the box shut and returned it to his pocket.

There was a touch of malice about his smile. "His lordship accepts. How could any man resist such a ... proposition?" He had the satisfaction of seeing the wild color flame in her cheeks. He turned to her stepfather. "When you are ready, Franklyn."

The other man wavered, then snatched up the dice box and threw.

"A three. Hardly good enough, I feel," mused his lordship.

He took his time, picked up the dice and returned them to the box. The tension became unbearable. Suddenly the dice rolled and came to rest under Mr. Franklyn's nose. The spots danced dizzily before his eyes as he stared stupidly.

Lord Mandersely's eyebrows rose. "That, I think, concludes that little charade!" He lifted a mocking, triumphant glance to the girl.

Lucia Mannering gave him back a long steady look, her underlip caught between small white teeth, the pulse in her throat beating furiously. Without uttering a word, she turned, and directing a glare barbed with pure hatred at her stepfather, she left the room.

Toby rushed to open the door, stammering sympathetic apologies, but she only shook her head. He came back to the table. Jasper Franklyn still sat as though carved out of stone, while Hugo, with an air of cool indifference, fastened his waistcoat and adjusted the set of his coat.

"You're mad, Hugo! That girl ain't like the stepfather, ye know. She's old Colonel Mannering's granddaughter, even if he don't own her. There was a frightful scandal—only son, Freddie, married some little Italian opera singer ... cut him off, just like that." Toby flicked his fingers and rattled on. "Don't know how you could do it anyway, subjecting that poor child to such ignominy!"

15

Hugo looked pained. "That *poor child* deliberately challenged me!"

"Nonsense! Why would she do a cork-brained thing like that?"

"How should I know, dear boy? I long ago gave up trying to fathom the workings of the female mind." He ran his fingers thoughtfully down the ribbon that held his glass. "I do know, however, that you gave her every opportunity to withdraw, and yet she deliberately provoked me. So if her pride is smarting, don't lay it at my door!"

Toby eyed his cousin balefully. "D'ye know, you've a damned nasty way with you sometimes, Hugo. Still, no harm done, eh? I vote we call it a night and toddle along."

Lord Mandersely yawned and rose languidly to his feet. "My dear Toby, I have been more than ready to leave, this hour past."

He ignored their host, who was by now collapsed across the table, and paused beside Mr. Thane.

"A word, Thane," he said softly. "No hint of this evening's events will be bandied abroad."

Mr. Thane looked contemptuous. "Your reputation will not suffer on my account, my lord."

The marquis was mildly amused. "It is not *my* reputation that concerns me, my friend." He nodded and walked from the room with Toby.

In the hallway they came to a sudden halt.

Beside the front door, wrapped in a dark cloak, stood Miss Mannering; a fur-trimmed hood emphasized charmingly the pallor of her face; at her side were piled several bandboxes.

16

"What the devil!" ejaculated Lord Mandersely. He strode toward her. "What new nonsense is this, ma'am?"

"No nonsense, my lord." She displayed that same infernal composure. "I did not wish to keep your lordship waiting. I have ordered your carriage to be brought around."

"Have you indeed?" The words were snapped out.

Toby was spluttering incoherently ". . . all a mistake, ma'am . . . do retire, I beg of you . . . never thought for a minute you'd taken it seriously. . . ."

She listened to him patiently and then turned to Lord Mandersely.

"Oh, go to your bed, child," he snapped. "The game is played out."

Those clear eyes never wavered from his face, though her words were addressed to his cousin.

"Captain Blanchard . . . I am very ignorant. Was there something wrong with the wager? It was perhaps not properly conducted?"

Toby blustered, "As to that, ma'am, the wager was quite in order, but it don't signify, d'ye see . . . Hugo ain't pressing his advantage."

"But *I am*," she insisted.

Toby dashed off, muttering something about rousing her stepfather.

Lord Mandersely, faced with Lucia Mannering's stubbornness, felt his anger rising by the minute. He longed to tear away that demure hood and wrap his fingers around her lovely white throat.

He said through clenched teeth, "Very well, Miss Mannering. You have called my bluff and have had a good laugh at my expense. Now, let us make an end of it."

He turned to where a wooden-faced footman waited to help him into his greatcoat—a magnificent affair of many capes.

"I am in earnest, my lord." For the first time there was a hint of passion in her voice. "You won the wager, I insist you must now take the responsibilty for your winnings."

"You insist!" He swung around. His voice cracked like a whiplash. "*You* insist! Nobody tells me what I must do, madam. *Nobody*!"

"I'm sorry." Her voice was low but intense. "But, oh, please, my lord, don't leave me here!"

Hugo's eyes narrowed, watching her tightly clasped hands. "Are you seriously suggesting that I should just take you away with me, now, tonight?"

"Yes."

"Without so much as a maidservant to chaperon you?"

"There is no one, sir, except perhaps one girl, and she will long since be abed."

"I see. And what the devil, pray, am I to do with you? You know that I live alone, but for my servants." He let the implication lie.

Two spots of color burned in the pale cheeks, and for a moment something like desperation flickered behind her eyes. Then her drooping figure straightened. There was only the merest tremor in her voice as she reaffirmed stubbornly, "I will not remain another night under this roof."

They glared at each other in silence until Toby returned.

"The damned fellow's snoring," he snorted. "A man who can't hold his liquor shouldn't drink!" He cocked an eyebrow at the two protagonists. "You agreed terms?"

Mandersely turned to his cousin, a sudden gleam in his eye. "It would appear that I am to take Miss Mannering home."

Toby was scandalized. "You can't do it, Hugo! Poor girl won't have a shred of name left if it gets about."

"Dear boy, you don't need to convince me!"

Toby turned. "Do beg of you, ma'am, reconsider!"

She stared back mutinously.

He tugged his cousin's to one side. The marquis removed his fingers and carefully smoothed the creases from his sleeve. Unfortunately Toby's idea of a whisper penetrated every corner of the hall.

"Daresay you won't like my speaking so, Hugo, you being seven years my senior . . ."

"Only seven years," marveled his lordship. "Unbelievable!"

"Don't hedge off, man!" Toby grinned. "Damnit, I'm not one to preach—least of all to you. It's well known your affairs are always discreetly conducted well away from Grosvenor Square. But that don't stop the rumors flying abroad. Take last summer— that little Portuguese opera dancer, the redhead who talked you out of those superb matched bays." He shook his head. "Shocking waste of good horseflesh. What was I saying? Ah, yes—well, Buffy Harcourt swore you had her tucked up in Grosvenor Square cozy as you please."

"Toby!"

"Eh?" He followed Hugo's quelling gaze and saw Miss Mannering, very pink, trying to look as though she hadn't heard every word. He stammered his apologies and assured her that she must take no notice of his rattling on. "Just the same, it won't do, m'dear—take my word for it. Have you no friend to whom you might go?"

She shook her head. "We lived abroad a lot, you see ... when my parents were alive ... I know no one in London."

"Then you'd best stay here, make the best of it. Daresay old Franklyn'll be sorry in the morn."

"No! I will not stay!"

The marquis regarded the stiff little figure in silence. At last, he turned to pick up his high-crowned beaver, set it upon his head, took up his gloves and his cane, and came to look down into her eyes. "Then there remains only one alternative, Miss Mannering."

Toby, in the act of struggling into his own greatcoat stared in open disbelief.

"No, Hugo! Sorry, but damnit, I won't let you do it." He turned and bowed to Miss Mannering with great decorum. "Profoundest apologies, my dear young lady. He don't mean any harm ... thing is, we're both a trifle foxed, d'ye see. ..."

"Speak for yourself, my boy" drawled his lordship. "For my part, my mind was never clearer."

Toby shook his head earnestly. "Only think so, Hugo . . . takes some people that way."

"I shall take Miss Mannering to Aunt Aurelia," the marquis explained gently.

Toby stared. "But . . . it's not far off midnight! The old dowager will be away to her bed long since. Can't go hammerin' on her door at this hour, dash it. Liable to give the old girl a nasty turn!"

"Nonsense. She's made of sterner stuff. Anyway, there will be no need to disturb my aunt. Saunders will do what is necessary. Saunders never goes to bed."

"All right, then, if you say so." Toby gave in cheerfully, glad to have the matter settled.

Lucia Mannering, however, was looking uncertainly from one to the other. "I wouldn't wish to put anyone out at this time of night. . . ."

The marquis found his irritability returning. He said shortly, "In that case, you had best remain here, ma'am."

"Oh dear!" She put her hands up to her face, trying to sort out her confused thoughts. "No . . . I will come."

"Good. Then let us go at once."

They left Toby at his lodgings en route, and when he had gone, it was unbearably quiet. There was no sound in the world, it seemed, but the creaking and rattling of the coach over the cobbles and the ring of the horses' hooves.

The marquis spoke not one word. He lounged in the corner of the coach, chin sunk deep in his chest, swaying easily with every lurch of the well-sprung vehicle.

When Portland Place was reached he roused himself with a sigh. He stepped down and held out a hand. "Come," he commanded.

Lucia obeyed, stumbling as a sudden and almost overpowering weariness possessed her. His hand tightened, steadying her.

"Tired, Miss Mannering?"

"A little, sir." Truth to tell, she was beginning to feel that the evening had been some hideous nightmare from which she would presently waken.

Lady Aurelia Springhope kept a porter on the door day and night, but since it was seldom that anyone called so late, he was in the habit of putting his feet up. He was soon roused, however, and was sent in search of Saunders.

On the threshold, Lucia stared, her weariness forgotten. Used as she was to Mr. Franklyn's modest hallway, this huge area of marble was breathtaking. A staircase rose in an elegant, sweeping curve; huge chandeliers hung from the ceiling; and adorning every space were trophies—extraordinary primitive statues, ornate masks and shields, objets d'art everywhere one looked.

The marquis observed her wide-eyed wonder with amusement. He put up his glass and swung slowly around "Hideous, ain't it?" he murmured. "My late lamented uncle was a much-traveled man and a compulsive collector. I am persuaded that, as his tastes became odder, my aunt came to dread his return. Ah, Saunders!" He turned as her ladyship's butler appeared as predicted, impeccably dressed and quite unruffled.

"This is Miss Mannering. She finds herself in an awkward situation. Accommodate her in one of my aunt's bedchambers."

Saunders heard him out without betraying the least surprise. He'd known Master Hugo far too long to be put out by his quirks. As a young 'un he was forever kicking up larks, and it was Saunders who usually got him out of trouble.

So now he inclined his head and said in his precise tones, "Certainly, Lord Hugo. Perhaps you would like to take the young lady into the library while I have a room prepared. Does her ladyship know of the arrangement? She has said nothing to me."

"Know? Of course she don't know. I didn't know myself until an hour ago. Don't worry, Saunders, I'll square it with my aunt tomorrow."

Lucia Mannering felt ready to sink. It was so easy to imagine what this stiff-backed old retainer would be thinking. Her cheeks flamed, and she was about to speak—to say that she would return home on the instant—when there was a sound at the head of the stairs.

"Aunt Aurelia!"

A strange apparition came slowly and stiffly down the stairs, until she stood above them, a tiny rotund figure in a voluminous dressing robe. A lace boudoir cap was perched atop a quantity of fading red hair, which hung over her shoulder in one long, heavy braid.

She fixed her nephew with a haughty glare, so like

his own that the family connection was unmistakable. A truly formidable lady.

"Well, nephew," she snapped querulously. "I trust you have a good reason for kicking up a dust and disturbing the peace of my house in the middle of the night."

"I had no wish to disturb you, aunt. Indeed, I am sorry for it. I merely came to crave a bed for Miss Mannering, who has been forced to leave her home."

Lady Springhope drew her rigid figure up straighter. Her nostrils quivered. "Pray enlighten me, Hugo. I have not moved much in social circles of late. Is it now become the fashion to quarter your *chère amie* on your family?"

A slow flush crept up under Hugo's skin. He spoke through his teeth. "That is unworthy of you, ma'am. I would never lay you open to the least breath of scandal. You have but to look at Miss Mannering to know she is not what you think her."

Lucia had reached her breaking point. She had been abominably ill-used, humiliated, bullied, and now this, the final insult. A horrid lump threatened to choke her as she gasped halfway between a laugh and a sob. "Oh, let us make an end of it, sir! I should not have come. I will go back!"

"Nonsense! There is no difficulty. My aunt will not refuse you shelter."

"Come here, Miss Mannering," demanded Lady Springhope.

Lucia looked as though she would refuse. Then slowly she walked to the foot of the stairs.

"Well, put your hood down, child. I can't see you properly if you hide beneath it."

Again she hesitated, and then she lowered her hood and stared defiantly back at the old lady.

Lady Springhope looked down into the hostile green eyes, opened wide against the threat of tears. She noted the shaded silvery-gold hair, the fine-boned fragility of the features, and for a moment something like recognition passed across her face. Then it was gone, and she grunted. "Hmp! Saunders?'

The old servant, who had faded discreetly into the background, now materialized silently.

"Saunders. Have the Rose Room made ready."

"I had already taken the liberty of having it prepared."

"Oh, had you?" She bent a fierce stare upon him and sniffed. "Hugo could ever wrap you around his little finger." She turned and said over her shoulder, "I shall send for you in the morning, Miss Mannering. And Hugo, you will call on me at midday. Good night to you."

Lucia remained staring after her until Lord Mandersely said behind her, "She is not as fearsome as she would have you think, Miss Mannering." She turned with a quick, nervous gesture, and he saw the weariness in her white face. "I will leave you in Saunders' good hands. I'm sure you are fit to drop." There was a suspicion of a smile lurking in his eyes. "You have had a lamentable evening. I wish you better dreams."

"Thank you." He swept out. She had to repress a

strong urge to run after him, to call him back. It was as though her only friend was deserting her—a ridiculous notion, she told herself dismally.

Saunders coughed, drawing her attention back. "If you would follow me, miss." They went up the staircase and along corridors that made her dizzy, until Saunders finally flung open a door. She hardly noticed the room, though she was surprised and gratified to find a fire burning in the grate and her bandboxes waiting for her.

"Is there anything you will be wanting, Miss Mannering? I fear all the young maidservants have retired, but I could rouse one of them. . . ."

"Oh, no!" she said quickly. "I wouldn't hear of it. You have been more than kind. I assure you there is nothing I need."

Saunders bowed and withdrew, leaving Lucia alone.

◆ Chapter 2 ◆

Lucia had thought to drop asleep the moment her head touched the pillow, but she was still tossing restlessly several hours later. Her tired brain was spinning, returning with relentless persistence to the enormity of the step she had taken. And the more she thought, the more she realized how glaringly open to misinterpretation were her actions.

In the darkness, the occasional flicker from the dying fire sent strange distorted shapes leaping onto the ceiling. Her face burned, and she pressed it into the cool, faintly perfumed silkiness of the sheets.

Gradually she slipped into that no-man's-land between sleeping and waking, pursued by fitful dreams—a confused jumble of frightening incidents, dominated by a kind of mock auction where Mr. Franklyn in a drunken frenzy was whipping up the bidding, led by a swaggering redhaired man who devoured her with bold, lustful eyes. Occasionally he would lean forward to caress her, allowing his hands to linger. The bidding rose higher, and so did her cries for help, but through it all, Lord Mandersely lay back in a chair, smiling and shaking his head.

Several times she started awake on the very edge of terror as the redhaired man, triumphant, lifted her, struggling and screaming, from the platform. . . .

She must have slept finally, for she awoke to find a young girl drawing back the curtains to let in the sunlight. For a moment she wondered where she was, and then, with a sinking feeling, she remembered. The maidservant turned and bobbed a cheerful curtsy. "Good morning, madam. Mr. Saunders hopes as you had a comfortable night and I'm to bring breakfast to you here, madam, as her ladyship never rises very early."

The rosy-cheeked girl was obviously agog to learn how they came to have a guest appear so mysteriously overnight. Lucia was obliged to hide a smile.

"Thank you," she said quietly. "It is very kind of Mr. Saunders. If I could just have something to drink. I am not hungry."

"You're not ill, are you, madam? You *do* look a bit peaked."

"I shall feel better directly," promised Lucia.

When she was dressed and as neat as she could make herself with the limited means at her disposal, she looked at her reflection in the dressing mirror, smoothing the pale green muslin with nervous fingers—it was the best of the few dresses she had hastily packed. Lord! The little maidservant was right. She looked positively sickly. She rubbed her cheeks vigorously and sat down to await the summons from Lady Springhope.

When it came, she was led back along the corridors of the previous night to her ladyship's room, where she was commanded to enter.

Lady Springhope was sitting bolt upright against a

bank of pillows in the middle of a huge four-poster bed, enveloped in a beautifully worked Indian shawl. She waved a hand toward a chair placed beside the bed.

"Come and sit down, child. Will you take some chocolate?"

Lucia declined politely.

Her ladyship turned to a thin, frosty-faced woman who hovered over her. "Then you may go, Parsons. I shall ring when I need you."

The woman nodded and cast a disparaging glance in Lucia's direction as she silently slid from the room.

Lady Springhope observed the pale young face, the dark circles under the eyes. "You do not look much rested, Miss Mannering. I trust we may soon be able to set you more at your ease."

"You are very kind, my lady."

"Before we speak of last evening, perhaps it would interest you to know that I am well-acquainted with your grandfather."

Lucia's eyes widened, and she half-rose in her chair. "My ... grandfather, ma'am?"

"Yes, miss, your grandfather. I also knew your father—he was my godson, in fact. I liked him very well, though he was as willfully stubborn as his parents. I was sorry to hear of his death."

"Thank you." Lucia forgot for a moment to be awed. "But, how did you know ... ?"

"That you were Freddie Mannering's daughter? Recognized you instantly, m'dear. You are the image of your late grandmother—God rest her. She was my dearest friend." Lady Springhope shook her head, "My word, had she lived, things would have been different! She would never have allowed that stupid rift to continue. But when a stiff-necked father and a hotheaded son clash head-on, with no softening influence . . ." She shrugged expressively. "However, that is past and too late to mend. What of you and your mother, child?"

Lucia Mannering clasped her hands in her lap. "My mother, too, passed away six months ago."

Lady Springhope made sympathetic noises. "Dear me, I didn't know that. I am sorry, my dear. You must be missing her."

"Oh, ma'am, you can have no idea how much I am missing her!"

It was like floodgates bursting open; the pentup emotion of months, once unleashed, would not be stopped. Lady Springhope let her talk, just uttering a word now and again.

"Mama was not at all as my grandfather imagined her. She came from a well-respected Neapolitan family. They were wiped out in a dreadful plague of cholera when she was just seventeen, all but herself and a small brother, who died two years later. There was little money, and with a sickly child to support, Mama had to find some means of earning a living. Her only talent was her voice, so she went into the opera."

Lady Springhope, watching the animation of the young face before her, was deeply moved. Tears rolled down Miss Mannering's cheeks unnoticed and unchecked. She was in the grip of a deep emotion.

"My father first saw her in Rome at the opera, when he was on the Grand Tour. They fell in love on sight and were married within a month." A wistful note crept into her voice. "They were still as much in love to the day he died.

"Grandfather cut off Papa's allowance the moment he heard of the marriage, and refused to have any dealings with him. We lived abroad a great deal. There seemed little point in coming home."

Memories came flooding back, of that vagabond existence with her dear, impractical father and her beautiful mama; of the times they had crept away at dead of night to avoid Papa's creditors.

"... of course it was wrong, but to my child's mind it was just a splendid lark! We were so happy, in spite of everything! Sometimes Mama would take engagements so that we might keep the tradesmen at bay. She had the loveliest voice...." Lucia's voice cracked.

Lady Springhope said quietly, "I do not think I heard how your father met his death. Would it pain you to speak of it?"

The clasped hands tightened until the knuckles showed white. "He was attempting to stop a bolting horse and wagon." Lucia gave an abrupt laugh that was half a sob. "It was ironic, for horses were ever his passion. The animal reared and kicked him in the chest, and two of his ribs punctured the lung. He died almost instantly in Mama's arms, and I think a part of her died with him."

Lucia looked up, her eyes swimming in tears. "She

31

was never quite herself afterward, else she would not have consented to marry Mr. Franklyn."

Lady Springhope's eyebrows rose, reminding Lucia vividly of her nephew. "Mr. Franklyn? Who, pray, is Mr. Franklyn?"

"We were in the north of England when Papa died, staying with friends. They kindly invited us to remain as long as we wished, and it was there that we met Mr. Franklyn. He was very rich and had grand ideas of entering London society. I believe . . ." Lucia hesitated, half-embarrassed. "I believe Mama encouraged him to think that she had entrée into the right houses. I can only imagine that, in her poor muddled mind, she was trying to provide a secure future for me."

"Neither of you thought of applying to your grandfather?"

"No, ma'am, we did not. We still had our pride, though we had little else!"

"Oh, fiddle!" The old lady shook her head irritably. "Pride! More sins have been committed in families in the name of pride! It is a thing I have no patience with!" She saw the mouth set rebelliously. "Oh, very well, miss, continue."

"There is little more to tell. They were married, and we came to London. I was never sure how Mama meant to carry off the deception, but in fact, it didn't matter. She fell ill almost at once, and in weeks she was dead. The doctor said it was a fever, but I believe she never recovered from the loss of my father."

There was a moment of silence, and then Lady

Springhope said quietly, "Well, Miss Mannering, you have had a sad time of it this last twelvemonth. It cannot have been a happy position in which to be left. I gained a distinct impression that you have no opinion of this Mr. Franklyn?"

Lucia said in a stilted voice, "That is true, my lady. I begged Mama not to marry him ... and lately I have even come to fear him." She looked at Lady Springhope with troubled eyes. "He invited gentlemen to the house regularly. I supposed that they came to play cards, but gradually I was made aware that there was another purpose to their visits. My stepfather began to insist that I make myself agreeable to his guests." Her voice sank to a whisper. "I realized I was being used as a kind of bribe, and would go to whoever was prepared to offer the greatest promise of advancement."

"But that is quite absurd! You must be mistaken!"

Lucia was crimson with shame. "I fear not. He wanted me off his hands, and if he could at the same time turn the affair to his advantage...."

"Could you not have sought shelter with friends?"

"I have no friends in London, and without money ..." She shrugged. "But I had resolved to seek employment, perhaps as a governess. I have been well educated and speak both Italian and French fluently." Her eyes lifted. "Do you think you might know of someone?"

"Later, child. For the moment I am more interested in the events of last night. I take it my nephew was one of the guests you mentioned. What I find puzzling is how they became acquainted. This Mr.

Franklyn does not sound in the least the kind of person Hugo would know."

"They had not, I think, met until last evening. Lord Mandersely was brought to the house by another young relation of yours—a Captain Blanchard."

Lady Springhope snorted. "Oh, young Toby's mixed up in this affair, is he? He is Hugo's cousin on his mother's side. A nice boy, but a bit of a rattle-pate."

"I found him most kind," said Lucia stiffly. "He was considerably more concerned for my welfare than . . ." She stopped, a hand flying to her mouth to check the slighting comparison she had been about to utter, but Lady Springhope only laughed.

"Than Mandersely, you were about to say, and I don't doubt you're right, m'dear. Think I don't know my own nephew? I am well aware that Hugo can be quite insufferable at times, but he ain't altogether to blame. His father, my brother, broke his neck riding to hounds some ten years since. Left Hugo with sole responsibility for his ailing mama and five younger brothers and sisters—a daunting enough prospect for a lively young man in his twenty-first year with all the world before him—and as if that were not enough, he found the estates had been most shockingly neglected."

Lucia found this picture of his lordship as a responsible family man intriguing to say the least.

Lady Springhope noted her surprise. "Don't let that air of indolence fool you, Miss Mannering. There's more to Hugo than meets the eye. Took him several years, and a considerable slice of the fortune willed to him by a doting godparent, to straighten things out, but he shouldered it all without a word of complaint. It has, however, left a layer of cynicism about him that makes him deuced unpopular in some quarters, but he goes his own way and don't give a damn what people say. The tabbies who tear his reputation to shreds would fall on his neck if only he would smile upon their spotty offspring."

She laughed abruptly. "Unfortunately, being Hugo, he despises the lot of 'em and don't scruple to show it! Just now he seems hell-bent on making up for those lost years, but I sometimes wonder if he finds much joy in the experience—which brings us back to last evening."

Lucia was silent, her lip caught pensively between small white teeth. "I don't think . . ."

Lady Springhope cast her an amused glance. "If you're thinking to shock me, my dear, you may be easy. I was married to the late earl at seventeen, and for years I set the town by the ears." Her eyes sparkled, and Lucia eyed her with new interest. It was easy to picture her as a young girl, tiny and vivacious, with hair which must have flamed most gloriously. "I delighted in doing the most shocking things, and though I have become a staid old dowager, there is still a little part inside me that yearns for excitement. So if you *can* bring yourself to tell me . . ."

Lucia began her halting explanation, her ladyship listened intently, with occasional grunts as the story progressed.

"I really left your nephew with little option," the

girl confessed with disarming honesty. "I challenged him quite deliberately."

"Why?" The question was shot out.

Lucia's brow creased earnestly. "I don't know. I spent most of the night trying to justify my actions. I can only say that it all happened so suddenly, I was terrified and humiliated. Mr. Franklyn was certainly very drunk, but his behavior seemed to indicate that he was determined to be rid of me . . . and if not by means of the wager . . . ?"

She rose abruptly and paced the room. "Do you know a man named Sir Gideon Benedict, ma'am?"

Lady Springhope sniffed. "A dangerous redhaired brute. He has a coarse virility that seems to attract the sillier type of woman. It is said that he can charm the birds off the trees. Nonetheless, there are some very unsavory rumors about him."

"As I thought," whispered Lucia. "He came often to the house, and he looked at me in such a way . . ." She shivered and colored with embarrassment. "I'm sure he was on the point of reaching some kind of agreement with Mr. Franklyn when he was called away."

She looked straight at Lady Springhope. "I dared not wait for his return. I took a chance on Lord Mandersely—he so obviously regarded me with complete indifference. I believe he sought only to teach me a sharp lesson." She smiled faintly. "He was none too pleased, in fact, to find himself saddled with me."

"That I can well imagine," said her ladyship dryly. "Well, Miss Mannering, you have given me a great deal to think about. We must see what can be done to mend matters." She tugged the bell pull vigorously. "Parsons will take you along to the small drawing room. I shall join you there presently."

The gaunt woman who had been in the room when she first arrived entered soundlessly and was given her instructions. In thin-lipped silence she escorted Lucia to a door, which she flung open with no more than a slight inclination of the head. With a feeling of acute depression, Lucia walked past her into the delightful cream and gold room.

In Grosvenor Square, Lord Mandersely had taken his customary early-morning ride and was enjoying a leisurely breakfast.

He looked up as the door opened to admit his secretary, who bade his employer a good morning and apologized for disturbing his breakfast. ". . . but there is a—er—gentleman called, who insists on speaking with your lordship."

Edward Jameson was a pleasant-faced young man of medium build, neatly if somewhat soberly clad in his habitual brown. His persistent uninterest in the vagaries of fashion was a constant source of pain to his employer, who now leaned back in his chair, put up his glass, and shuddered delicately.

Edward Jameson bore the unspoken censure with equanimity. He knew that such affectations masked a brain far keener than his own.

"About the caller, sir?" he queried again.

The marquis sighed. "I leave him to you, Edward.

Get rid of him. No one who is anyone would dream of calling at such an hour."

He rose languidly to his feet and indicated his riding clothes, a faint gleam in his eye. "Besides, I must change. I really cannot call upon my aunt improperly dressed."

Edward held out the calling card. "The gentleman was most insistent that you would see him, my lord."

The marquis shot him a keen glance and took the card from him, reading it without expression. He walked across to the fireplace and stood, with one arm resting easily along the mantelshelf, staring down into the flames.

"Edward?' he probed, without looking up. "When I came in last evening, was I very badly foxed?"

The young man weighed his words with care. "I think not," he said with simple truthfulness. "I knew you had been drinking, of course, for I know the signs. But in the three years I have been with you, my lord, I have never seen you the worse for drink."

Mandersely looked up quizzically. Seeing that his secretary was perfectly serious, he flashed him a sudden, unexpectedly boyish grin. "You're a good fellow, Edward. I must strive to be more worthy of you."

He straightened and tossed the card into the fire, watching it curl up in the flames. "Where have you put our Mr. Franklyn?"

"He has been shown into the crimson salon, my lord."

The marquis strode from the room and across the

wide hall, tiled in white Italian marble. A footman sprang to attention and flung open the salon door.

Mr. Franklyn had been subjecting the room to a close inspection. He turned as the door opened, looking very much under the weather, and greeted Lord Mandersely with unctuous overenthusiasm.

"I have been admiring your furnishings, my lord —the paintings, the porcelain—quite exquisite. In fact, the whole house would seem impressive, most impressive."

Manderely inclined his head. "You are most kind. Shall I call my butler? He would be pleased to take you on a conducted tour." He watched the other man color up. "No? You did not then call this morning simply to admire my house?"

Mr. Franklyn stirred uncomfortably. "Well, no. . . . To be frank, my lord, I have come on a matter of some delicacy. Still . . . as men of the world, I'm sure we can come to some amicable agreement."

His lordship settled on the edge of a table. He sat swinging one leg gently to and fro, evinced an air of polite interest, and waited.

Mr. Franklyn looked even more uneasy. He coughed. "I am told, my lord, that my stepdaughter left my house last night in your company. Since she has not returned, and is, after all, little more than a child, I naturally feel a fatherly concern for her welfare."

The marquis put up his glass and regarded his top boot thoughtfully. "Tell me, Franklyn, would you call that a flaw in the leather—just there?" He indicated. "I very much fear it is."

His companion seemed stunned by the total irrelevance of the question. "Good God, man! What has your boot to do with anything? We are talking of my stepdaughter."

Mandersely sighed. "How much do you remember of last night, Franklyn?"

He was rewarded by the obvious discomforture of his visitor, who began to bluster "... best forgotten ... all acted somewhat rashly...."

"Very wise. It is forgotten."

"B-but my stepdaughter, sir?"

"Is safe, sir!"

Franklyn exploded. "No, damnit, it's not good enough, my lord. There is her good name to be considered."

"Your concern is touching, if somewhat tardy!" There was an unmistakable sneer in the gentle voice. "However, you may set your mind at rest. Miss Mannering's good name will not be tarnished."

"Ah!" A subtle change came over Mr. Franklyn. He almost purred. "Well, there's no denying she has been a foolish child, but I'll warrant you'll not be disappointed, my lord. She has been well brought up ... comes of good stock, ye know. I'm even prepared to make her a handsome settlement, though she ain't strictly my responsibility."

A slight frown creased Lord Mandersely's brow. "You've lost me, Franklyn."

"You *are* offering for her, my lord?"

One eyebrow rose fractionally. "Now, whatever gave you *that* idea?"

"It's the only honorable thing to do," exclaimed

Franklyn. "Her grandfather is an important man. True, he ain't had anything to do with her, but he'd doubtless change his tune fast enough if he was to learn that she'd been taken from her home and possibly ravished—"

He got no farther. The marquis hardly appeared to move, yet Mr. Franklyn suddenly found himself seized by the throat in a grip that lifted him off his feet. His hands clawed the air as the slim fingers tightened remorselessly in the folds of his cravat. His bloodshot eyes bulged with terror.

Through the distressing noises in his head, the marquis' voice came and went, low and menacing. "Insufferable cur! Do you dare to threaten me? I should wring your scheming neck." He was being shaken as a dog shakes a rat. "Do you think for one moment that anyone would listen to a social-climbing little toady like you?"

He was released with an abruptness that sent him sprawling, bringing one of his lordship's beautiful gilt chairs crashing to the ground.

Mr. Franklyn lay for a moment, stupefied, before scrambling to his knees in a most undignified manner, pulling at his cravat, and gulping in great gasps of air. His face was purple, and his wig had slipped ludicrously over one ear.

The marquis watched him with cold, dispassionate eyes.

"You'll answer for this, my lord," Franklyn croaked.

He received no answer, beyond a slight curl of the lip. He clambered to his feet and set himself to rights. His voice quivered with fury. "I demand satisfaction."

"You may demand all you like, my friend," said his lordship icily. "I have no intention of gratifying you. I strongly advise you to return home at once. You don't look at all well." He moved to the fireplace and pulled the bell rope.

At once the door was opened by the impassive footman.

"Mr. Franklyn is leaving," said Lord Mandersely.

Franklyn glared from servant to master and knew himself beaten. "Very well, my lord, but you haven't heard the last of this. I'll warrant you don't shift that chit of a girl as easily as you think to get rid of me!" An unpleasant smile crossed his face. "I declare, I could laugh when I think of her cunning—playing hard to get all these weeks past, and then she wraps you up as neat as ninepence."

Mandersely's hand stilled in the act of taking a pinch of snuff. His eyes narrowed. Then he calmly inhaled and snapped the snuffbox shut. As Mr. Franklyn reached the door, he was halted.

"One small thing." His lordship spoke softly. "If one word of what has passed either last night or this morning is leaked abroad, I shall make you very sorry. And, Franklyn . . ." The voice hardened. "For your information, I am no 'Johnny Raw.' Your stepdaughter entered this house. I took her straight to my aunt in Portland Place."

Franklyn threw him a look of hatred and pushed past the footman without another word.

The marquis remained standing in the middle of

the room, his face wiped clean of all expression. Slowly he opened his clenched hand; the gold-filigree snuffbox was crushed flat. With a gesture of disgust he flung it away.

◆ Chapter *3* ◆

The marquis reached Portland Place just before noon. Saunders informed him that her ladyship was not yet about but that Miss Mannering was in the small drawing room, if he should wish to go up. Hugo thanked him and made his leisurely way up the staircase.

He found Miss Mannering seated near the window, leafing aimlessly through the pages of a book. She was trying to bolster up her courage for the coming interview with Lord Mandersely and prayed that Lady Springhope would be there to lend her support.

Her head lifted and at the sight of the tall figure she almost panicked. She forced herself to put the book down without hurry, and stood up. "Good morning, my lord," she said quietly.

In the cold light of day he looked even less approachable. The elegance of his dress made her very conscious of the shortcomings of the green muslin, and she was unaware that, with her hair simply drawn back from her face, she presented an entirely fresh and charming picture.

Lord Mandersely inclined his head and subjected

her to an unhurried scrutiny. "Good morning, Miss Mannering. I trust you slept well?"

"Quite well, I thank you, sir." She turned her head away to avoid his too observant eyes.

"How fortunate!" As always a thin vein of sarcasm ran beneath his words. "I was so afraid you might have too much on your mind. I am overjoyed to find my fears unfounded."

Insufferable man! Lucia's lips tightened. "I daresay it would please you to find that I had passed a miserable night."

He looked pained. "My dear Miss Mannering, I should be very sorry to know that you had slept badly." He paused. "Though I believe it often *is* the case when one's plans are unexpectedly overset."

His voice made her uneasy. "Should that remark have some special significance, my lord?"

"It might." His sleepy gaze was fixed on her with a curious intentness. "I received a visitor this morning. Your stepfather."

"Mr. Franklyn! Don't say that he came to apologize? I cannot believe it."

"To apologize—no. His visit was more in the nature of a threat." Her bewilderment increased. "He accused me in so many words of removing his stepdaughter—an innocent young girl—from his protection, and demanded an *amende honorable*."

Lucia's green eyes widened.

"In short, he proposed marriage as the only possible solution."

"Oh no!" Distress mingled with the contempt in her voice. "Oh, how like my stepfather to seize the chance of allying himself to a lord! He must have been in a fury to find his ambition thwarted."

"He was not pleased!" The marquis paused. "It crossed my mind that he might not be alone in his displeasure?"

"I do not understand you, sir."

"I think you do, madam," he said softly, "but I will rephrase so that there may be no misunderstanding. Suppose I offer you, now, my hand in marriage?"

She slowly turned crimson as bewilderment gave way to indignation and finally to anger. "I thank you for the *honor* sir." Her voice shook. "But I did not escape from one tyrant in order to tie myself to another. How typically arrogant and conceited of you to suppose me capable of such deviousness. You are just like all of your kind."

Lord Mandersely's eyes were hard and he toyed absently with the black ribbon of his quizzing glass. "Are you, then, so familiar with my kind?"

"Oh yes, my lord!" There was a world of scorn and bitterness in her words. "In the months since my mother's death, Mr. Franklyn has been busy courting the nobility and pseudo-nobility, and in that time I have been most shamefully used, I have been paraded for inspection, subjected to every excess of overfamiliarity you can name, in the hopes that one of these 'fine gentlemen' might honor me with his favors in return for certain considerations!"

Hugo's brows drew together. "And so you really class me among this riff and raff?"

"Oh, I am well aware that you consider yourself a

cut above ordinary mortals! Your air of lofty disdain did not go unnoticed last night."

"But then, you see," he explained softly, "*I* like to choose on whom I bestow my favors. I do not like being maneuvered."

Lucia flinched at the rebuke. "Your scruples did not prevent you from accepting my stepfather's wager?"

He strode across the room and towered over her. "Let us have plain speaking, madam. It was your challenge I accepted, *as you intended I should!* Did you realize what you were doing—how it must appear? Or did you simply not care?"

His closeness was overpowering, but Lucia stood her ground. "No, sir, I did not care! To be, as it were, put up for auction was the final humiliation. At that moment it seemed any change could only be for the better!"

"Then it was well for you that I did not exact my dues in full."

"Oh, I do indeed thank you for your gallantry and consideration!" Her voice quivered with heavy sarcasm. "But then, I was not really to your taste in the first place, was I, my lord?"

His expression frightened her, yet she flung her head back defiantly, her eyes blazing with unshed tears. At every moment she expected he would strike her, and tensed herself in readiness. The silence stretched interminably, until a sharp voice broke the spell.

"I daresay, nephew, that you will have the good

manners to greet me when you find it convenient to do so."

Lady Springhope had entered the room quite unnoticed. The marquis spun around, flushing darkly. "Aunt Aurelia! I did not hear you come in."

"That does not surprise me!" said his aunt dryly, looking from one to the other. Lucia turned away to dash a hand across her eyes and regain her composure.

The tiny, stately lady came across the room and settled herself on her favorite sofa, smoothing her striped bombazine skirts to her liking. "I take it you two have been brawling?"

When there was no reply, she continued tartly, "Well, you can come down off your high ropes, both of you. I'll not have it! Miss Mannering, come and be seated." She tapped the sofa with an imperious gesture of her closed fan, and Lucia dutifully obeyed. The marquis took up his favorite stance at the fireplace, silent and brooding.

"Now, Hugo, this child has explained to me the events of last evening, which I find utterly incomprehensible. While she has made every effort to excuse your behavior—"

"Has she, egad!" ejaculated his lordship, directing a quick, frowning glance upon Miss Mannering's bent head.

"Don't interrupt, Hugo! As I was saying, Miss Mannering may find excuses for you—I am bound to say I can find none. But then, young people today behave generally with a lack of finesse that would have been unthinkable in my young day." She encountered a particularly sanguine stare from her nephew. "Well, Hugo? You wish to say something?"

His eyes opened a little wider. "No, ma'am."

"Liar! You know you are longing to throw my own youthful indiscretions in my teeth."

Hugo's lips twitched. "Nothing of the kind, dear aunt. I would never be so *ungallant*." He laid a curious emphasis on the final word, and Lucia lifted her head to find his mocking eyes upon her. She stared back, tight-lipped.

Lady Springhope did not miss this little charade, there was a gleam in her eye as she continued. "Good! Because we are not here to discuss my past, but Miss Mannering's future."

"Does that mean you will help me, ma'am? Do you perhaps know of someone in need of a governess?"

"No, child, I do not. And I am bound to say I can see no possibility of your obtaining such a post." Lady Springhope watched the light die out of the young face; she patted Lucia's hand kindly. "You are too pretty m'dear. No wife in her right mind would employ you. Ain't that so, Hugo?"

"Undoubtedly," the marquis lifted a mocking brow.

"So I have decided what I am going to do," she continued with an air of decision. "I shall write to your grandfather."

"No!" Lucia sprang to her feet.

Lady Springhope drew herself up haughtily. "I beg your pardon, miss?"

"I am sorry, ma'am! That sounded ungracious. Indeed I did not mean to seem so. But you must see how impossible it is!"

"No, frankly, I do not."

The young girl was in a state of agitation. "For almost nineteen years my grandfather has denied my existence. I cannot—will not—crawl to him now!"

Lady Springhope exchanged glances with her nephew and received an eloquent shrug.

"You are very bitter, Miss Mannering."

"Yes, ma'am, I am. Do I not have cause?"

Her ladyship smiled sadly. "Perhaps. But it is so easy for the young to be intolerant. Have you never thought of the cost to your grandfather?"

Lucia frowned.

"My dear child, all these years your little family have been together, loving one another, sharing, enjoying things together, while he, in a fit of anger not entirely unjustified. . . ." She held up a hand to forestall the ready protest. "I repeat, not entirely unjustified. Your father behaved with a total lack of consideration. However, that is neither here nor there; the fact remains that your grandfather cut himself off from all the pleasure you would have brought him."

"It was his own doing, ma'am. One word—that was all it needed!"

"Ah, but that is the hardest word of all to utter, my dear. Your grandfather is—always has been—a proud man. You will find as you get older that it becomes increasingly difficult to admit to being in the wrong."

Lady Springhope searched the stubborn young face before her. "What I am trying to say is that he

50

is now an old man, and I fear, a sick man. He is all alone in the world except for your Aunt Addie, and I think he sometimes finds her more of a trial than a comfort.

"Of course, he is devilishly proud, and has, as you say, denied you all these years." She paused. "But could you not find it in your heart to at least offer him a chance to mend matters?"

There was a long silence. Lucia looked uncertainly at Lady Springhope, her eyes wide and troubled. She had never thought of her grandfather as a flesh-and-blood person; he was that nebulous creature—who had denied her father his rightful place in the world. Trying to picture him now as Lady Springhope had described him, she found it impossible to whip up her usual passion of indignation.

She said huskily, "You have made me ashamed, ma'am. I will do whatever you think best."

"Good girl!" Lady Springhope beamed at her. "I shall draft a letter to Rupert this very day."

"I had quite forgotten your connections with the Mannerings," drawled Hugo. "Now I recall, wasn't there some talk of the old colonel being one of your flirts?"

"Really, Hugo!" she admonished, sighed nostalgically. "Dear me, that was a very long time ago, before he met his beloved Marianne. From the moment she came on the scene, there was never anyone else. But though I haven't seen him for many years, he had ever a soft spot for me."

She patted Lucia's hand. "Of course, nothing is certain, my dear. I cannot vouchsafe that Rupert will agree to a meeting, but you shall stay with me in the meanwhile."

"You are being very kind to me, ma'am." Lucia smiled tremulously.

"Stuff, child! I declare, I was becoming very dull and stay-at-home, with my Maria married and moved away into Gloucestershire." She beamed. "So, my dear Miss Mannering—no, I cannot be calling you that if we are to be together. Lucia, is it not? You don't mind?"

"No, I should like it."

"Good. I really believe everything is going to work out splendidly. You may go down to Culliford Cross to spend the summer with your grandfather, and return to me in the autumn." Lady Springhope turned to her nephew. "You have not forgotten, Hugo, that your sister is to come to me in the autumn. I promised your dear mama that she should come as soon as she passed her eighteenth birthday."

The marquis groaned and covered his eyes with one slim white hand. "Good God! I shall arrange to go on a very long journey!"

"You will do no such thing! You will stay here and play your part in helping to establish your sister. If you give your mind to it, I am sure you should be able to find her a suitably eligible husband."

"Not I!" retorted Hugo bluntly. "I'm not saying that I wouldn't be glad to see Hetty safely leg-shackled, but in all conscience, I wouldn't wish her on my worst enemy!"

"Oh stuff! Hetty is just a normal, high-spirited

girl. I am sure, my dear Lucia, that the two of you will get along famously."

A small frown had gathered on Lucia's brow. "But what if my grandfather is obdurate, ma'am? I must then find some means of earning a living."

"I have quite decided, my love. Even if the worst should happen, you shall still come to me, for your dear late grandmama's sake and because Freddie was my godson. He was too stubborn to accept any help from me when he was alive, but I would like to think he might approve my helping you now. However," she added complacently, "I do not think Rupert will refuse me."

Saunders came soft-footed into the room and made his way to Lady Springhope's side to inform her quietly that there was a young person below, come with a large portmanteau for Miss Mannering.

"Indeed!" Her ladyships eyebrows rose. "Then have it conveyed at once to Miss Mannering's room." She turned to Lucia and said dryly, "It would seem that your Mr. Franklyn has wasted little time in washing his hands of you."

"That is probably my doing," murmured Hugo. "I had a brush with him this morning."

"And gave him swift dismissal, I trust?"

"I did!" His lordship's eye rested meditatively on Lucia's face. "I do not think Miss Mannering will be troubled any further."

Saunders inquired what he should do about the young person. "She appears to be in a distressed state. I gather she has been dismissed, my lady."

Lucia sprang up. "It must be Chloe—poor child.

She undoubtedly spoke her mind on my behalf, and
he's turned her off for spite."

"In that case, my dear, you had best keep her,"
suggested Lady Springhope with a twinkle.

"Oh, but ... Could I? May I tell her so, ma'am?
She would be so grateful. Thank you!" Impulsively
Lucia bent to kiss the rouged and scented cheek be-
fore whisking from the room.

In the silence following the closing of the door,
the marquis eyed his aunt with a kind of lazy,
amused indulgence. "I do hope you realize, dear
aunt, just what you are taking on!"

Lady Springhope came out of a bemused reverie
to glare at him. She produced her handkerchief and
blew her nose fiercely.

Lucia followed Saunders down the staircase. He
led her to a small back parlor, where she found a
large, rawboned girl of about sixteen sobbing noisily
into her apron. Beside her was a pathetically small
bundle, which obviously contained all her worldly
possessions. The sight of her dear Miss Mannering
brought on a fresh paroxysm of weeping, it took Lucia several minutes to calm her and tell her of Lady
Springhope's kind suggestion. Chloe's jaw dropped
and her eyes, blotched with tears, opened saucer
wide.

"You mean ... stay here ... with you, miss?" She
swallowed on a hiccup.

"Yes."

"Oh, miss!"

"Well, then ..." Lucia turned uncertainly to

Saunders, who took instant command of the situation.

'You come with me, my girl. Mrs. Barchester, the housekeeper, will see you; she will explain your duties, inform you of house rules and"—his glance swept over her—"provide you with suitable clothing."

Chloe bobbed him a nervous curtsy. With a loud sniff and a last reluctant glance back at her beloved Miss Mannering, she picked up her bundle and followed Saunders from the room.

Lucia wandered back into the main hall, trying to quell the little bubbles that kept welling up inside her. She stared with renewed fascination at the eccentric collection of bric-a-brac, which seemed no less bizarre in broad daylight.

Before a fearsome figure of a native warrior, complete with spear and feathered headdress, she paused. On a sudden impulse she stepped back and swept him a deep, formal curtsy, and rose to find a very young footman staring at her openmouthed. She flashed him her most dazzling smile and walked up the wide staircase, choking back a strong desire to collapse into giggles.

At the drawing-room door she stopped, suddenly shy. Then she lifted her head and went in.

In her absence, Captain Blanchard had arrived. He was standing near the fireplace in conversation with Lord Mandersely. He swung around on hearing the door and came across to her, pleasure lighting his nice, honest face. He lacked the more stylish elegance of his cousin, but Lucia found nothing to quarrel with in his appearance.

"Miss Mannering! I came along to see how you did!" He smiled down at her, and his brilliant blue eyes crinkled at the corners. "Yes, you are already looking much more the thing. Lady Springhope has been telling me of her plans for you; I couldn't be more pleased!"

He looked sheepish and tugged at his cravat. "I came also to offer my apologies."

"Apologies, Captain Blanchard?"

"The fact is, ma'am, I believe I was more than a trifle foxed last night . . . don't wish to revive painful memories for you, but . . . I hope nothing I might have said or done was in any way offensive." He appeared immensely relieved to have got this speech off his chest.

Lucia smiled at him. "You may be easy, Captain Blanchard. *Your* conduct was unfailingly courteous and in every way that of a gentleman."

Lord Mandersely's gentle, sardonic voice completed the inference. "While I, my dear Toby, as a mere nobleman, was not bound by any such ridiculously conventional notions."

"Eh?" Toby stared at his cousin in disbelief, then at Lady Springhope, who was chuckling with delight. He followed the direction of their gaze back to Miss Mannering, now turned rather pink.

"Oh, I see!" He grinned. "You two still wrangling, are you?"

"Not at all," said Lucia primly. "And I think it

most unfair of his lordship to throw up at me something that was said in the heat of the moment."

The marquis laughed suddenly. "Oh, come, Miss Mannering, let us cry pax."

"Certainly, sir, if that is what you wish." Lucia regarded him in silence for a moment, her head on one side, and then her innate honesty forced her to a decision. "I believe I must owe you an apology, my lord."

His eyebrow quirked upward.

"I . . . I am only too well aware how much I am in your debt, and I do indeed thank you for your . . . your forbearance last night." She was very conscious of his ironic scrutiny as she continued with heightened color. "Unfortunately, this morning you provoked me into losing my temper, and I fear I said a number of things that would have been better left unsaid. For that I am indeed sorry."

The marquis stood looking down at her in silence, and then a warm smile lit his sleepy eyes. "That was well done, Miss Mannering; you put me to shame." He held out his hand. "Come—shall we agree to forget the events of the last twenty-four hours and begin again?"

"Gladly, my lord," said Lucia shyly. His handclasp was firm and cool.

"Good girl!" Still with the ghost of a smile, he flicked her cheek lightly with one long slim finger. "And by the by, little spitfire," he murmured, "try to keep that temper in check. I don't know if you realize quite how close you came to feeling the weight of my hand. Next time you might not be so lucky!"

◆ Chapter 4 ◆

The days passed for Lucia in a haze of happiness. Memories of Bruton Street faded to an occasional bad dream, and her naturally buoyant spirits reasserted themselves.

She saw little of Lord Mandersely, though Captain Blanchard became a fairly regular caller. In fact, Portland Place suddenly became a very popular venue. Some of the visitors were old friends of Lady Springhope's, but many others left cards, drawn simply by curiosity concerning her ladyship's young protégée, who was rumored to be Freddie Mannering's child.

Society had a long memory where scandals were concerned, and Lucia's arrival on the scene was just the fillip needed to stimulate gossiping tongues. Fortunately, Lucia was so overjoyed to be coming alive again, she was blissfully unaware that a certain amount of malicious gossip was mingled with the more kindly interest shown in her.

Lady Springhope had insisted on replenishing Lucia's limited wardrobe. She waved away all protests, declaring that a few dresses were neither here nor there, and added dryly that the few she did possess were scarcely adequate for her present needs.

This Lucia could not deny. She had long since

outgrown most of her older dresses, and the few that remained had required all her considerable skill and ingenuity with a needle to maintain any degree of freshness and fashion. Mr. Franklyn had been mean, for all his wealth. He was willing to invest in gowns like that dreadful one she had been obliged to wear on that fateful evening when she had met Lord Mandersely, but in every other respect he had kept her woefully short.

So she gave herself up happily to the task of choosing, for almost the first time in her life, exactly what she liked. Also, there was the small allowance Lady Springhope had pressed upon her, a mere trifle, she insisted, for the purchasing of knickknacks, but to Lucia, it was riches.

With Chloe in attendance, she spent countless hours haunting the modish shops of New Bond Street and Piccadilly, delighting in the absurdities of dress and manners to be encountered in this most fashionable of quarters; the fops tottering on high, mincing heels, their faces heavily painted, wearing bizarre polka dots and stripes, and collars so high that their wearers could not possibly see where they were going.

The shops were in themselves a delight; she lingered over a length of ribbon here, a fine lace trimming there, lovingly selecting a pair of pale yellow kid gloves or, when she felt truly extravagant, perhaps a book.

With her thoughts lost in her latest purchase, a brand-new copy of Mr. Scott's *Marmion*, Lucia emerged from Hatchard's bookshop in Piccadilly one morning, straight into the arms of a passing gentleman, and was dismayed to find herself held fast.

An odiously familiar voice with just a hint of brogue said softly, "Why, Lucia—darling girl! If this isn't a happy coincidence!"

Time rolled back; her heart began to beat with a heavy thud. She looked up, into the mocking eyes of Sir Gideon Benedict.

"Please, Sir Gideon, release me this instant!" she commanded coldly. "People are staring!"

"And why wouldn't they stare? The men will all be wishing they were in my place, and the women ... sure, who knows what women will be thinking?"

He let her go, and she stepped backward instinctively. He smiled. "As I said, a happy coincidence. I am to visit your stepfather this very evening. There is a matter I must settle with all speed—a matter which would be settled by now, had I not been called away." His glance moved boldly over her. "I confess I am impatient for its conclusion!"

Lucia suppressed a shudder. She looked around swiftly to reassure herself of Chloe's presence, peering goggle-eyed from behind a mountain of small parcels. It was ridiculous to be so unnerved in a public place, yet it took every ounce of self-possession to say calmly, "Then I wish you luck, Sir Gideon. I shall not see you there, for I am no longer at Bruton Street."

He was suddenly still, watchful. "Why? How is this? Nothing was said before I went away."

"It was ... unexpected. I am now staying in Portland Place, with Lady Springhope."

For a fleeting instant wild fury distorted the heavy features. "Mandersely's aunt. I see!"

"Lady Springhope is a particular friend of my grandfather," Lucia said quickly—too quickly. The mocking smile returned, but this time it didn't reach the hard eyes.

"So! It seems I must change my plans."

She could scarcely breathe. "I don't understand you, sir."

"Oh, I think you do, fair Lucia. I think we understand each other very well!" Lucia couldn't look away. His voice sank to a vehement whisper. *"You are mine!"*

Oh God, she must get away! Her limbs felt paralyzed. And then, as if in answer to her prayer, a voice hailed her; the reassuring figure of Captain Blanchard was bearing down on them. Lucia could have fallen on his neck.

"Miss Mannering! Here's a lucky chance. I have just called at Portland Place and found you were gone out. I came along here in hopes of finding you."

For the first time, he noticed her companion, and his expression altered. He nodded curtly. "Your servant, Benedict."

"Captain Blanchard!" Sir Gideon's voice was gently derisive. "I might have guessed you would be lurking nearby. In affairs concerning your cousin, you are seldom far away."

Lucia saw Toby's jaw tighten and said quickly, "Captain Blanchard, I have completed my purchases. Would you be kind enough to see me home?"

She tugged at his sleeve, her eyes pleading with

him not to make trouble. Toby swallowed his anger and smiled gently down at her. "Gladly, Miss Mannering." He turned. "We bid you good day, Benedict."

Sir Gideon bowed with exaggerated courtesy. "I am desolated. But we shall meet again, my dear Lucia."

She swung on her heel and left him standing. With Chloe half-running behind them, juggling with her packages, Toby strode along at Lucia's side, muttering words like "unscrupulous" and "scoundrely rogue." Finally, he said with a rueful grin, "Sorry, Miss Mannering! Let us forget the creature. Come, take my arm."

Lucia did so, and he exclaimed, "Why, my dear, you are trembling! Benedict really rattled you, didn't he? You should have let me plant him a facer!"

She laughed shakily. "Oh, it is quite ridiculous, the way that man affects me! I can't explain it."

"I can. The fellow's a rotten egg!"

"I daresay you are wondering how I come to know such a man?"

"None of my business, m'dear," he said gently. "Though he ain't one I'd recommend as a friend."

Haltingly she told him what she had told Lady Springhope.

Toby was incensed. "I tell you what, dear girl. Shouldn't venture out on foot—even with your maid. Use the carriage. Her ladyship won't mind."

"Oh, come now, Captain Blanchard!" Lucia was

half-amused by his earnestness. "What could Sir Gideon possibly do in a public thoroughfare?"

"Dont' know, m'dear," said Toby bluntly. "But I know what he's capable of."

"He is really so bad?"

"Oh, I'll grant he can be as charming as you please, but there's a side of his character that don't bear investigation. 'Tis rumored that he heads a paid army of cutthroats and ruffians, not to mention young bloods out for a little sport, robbing any poor traveler caught out alone, often leaving them near-dead."

"But that is dreadful!"

"Oh, that's only the half of it. He is known to own a number of the brothels in the region of Covent Garden and Pall Mall; makes a tidy profit out of procuring poor unfortunates to stock them. . . ." He became aware of her shocked expression and blushed to the roots of his fair hair. "Miss Mannering . . . I do beg your pardon! Quite unforgivable of me to soil your ears with such tattle."

"Don't be nonsensical!" scoffed Lucia. "Tell me—how is he allowed to get away with such wickedness?"

"Often wondered about that myself. Of course, hearsay ain't evidence, and he has some pretty influential friends. Shouldn't wonder if he don't have something on them; blackmail would fit with all the rest. He's certainly never short of funds, and it don't come from his family. The estates in Ireland are known to be in a poor way."

Lucia was silent, appalled but not surprised.

"Tell you what, m'dear," said Toby diffidently. "Don't know how much longer I shall be around . . . off abroad any day, d'ye see, but when the army isn't claiming my time, I'd be happy to appoint myself your escort."

Lucia was touched and said she would accept gladly, but only if he was sure it would not be an imposition, and that he would promise to tell her if it became so. Thus, under the surprised and benevolent eye of Lady Springhope the pair became fast friends.

Sir Gideon crossed their path so often that coincidence must be ruled out, but he made no further attempt to engage Lucia's attention. His constant presence, however, made her nervous, as no doubt it was meant to do. She knew that he was only waiting, biding his time.

Lord Mandersely they saw not at all. Lucia did not know whether to be glad or sorry; on balance she decided that she was glad. There had been an abrasive quality about their brief encounters that she had found decidedly unsettling.

Toby, missing his cousin, however, finally ran him to earth late one night in White's, deep in a game of faro. He wandered across to the table. "Hugo, there you are! I had given up hope of finding you."

"Well, now you have done so, be easy, I pray you, dear boy," sighed his lordship without raising his eyes from the table.

Toby grinned, unabashed, and stood watching play.

"Do you care to sit in, Blanchard?" Alvanley asked good-naturedly.

"Not I!" retorted Toby. "A captain's pay don't run to your kind of stakes!"

"Against your cousin's luck, I don't blame you," George Brummel murmured with feeling.

Play finally broke up, with the marquis running out a comfortable winner, and as the others drifted away, Hugo lit up a cigar and lounged back in his chair, eyeing Toby through the curling smoke. "Well, dear boy, here I am. You wanted me?"

"Not really. I just haven't seen you ... wondered if you had been away."

Hugo looked faintly surprised. "As a matter of fact, Edward and I have been spending a few days down at Mandersely Court, going over the estate accounts with old Blenkinsop. I might have suggested your joining us ... Mama would have been pleased to see you"—he paused significantly—"but I believed you to be fully occupied."

"Who, me?" Toby was mystified.

"Miss Mannering, my boy. I hear you are now become quite inseparable."

"Oh, that!"

"Are felicitations in order yet?" queried Hugo softly.

"Good Lord! It ain't that kind of relationship!"

"You surprise me," murmured his cousin. "I have been expecting almost hourly to learn of your approaching nuptials."

Toby groaned. "Stop it, Hugo, you're roasting me!

I'm dashed fond of Lucia, of course . . . but, well, you know me. . . ."

"Indeed I do, dear boy." Hugo's expression was bland. "But wonder, does Miss Mannering?"

"Yes, of course she does! Lucia wouldn't expect . . . she doesn't . . . Toby broke off in confusion, to see Hugo's shoulders shaking with silent laughter. "Hugo, you devil! You *are* roasting me!"

He could not put this conversation out of his head; it kept coming back to plague him, so that when he next met Lucia, he was decidedly edgy.

They had arranged to take Lady Springhope to Vauxhall Gardens to enjoy the music. There, to her delight, she came upon her dear friend Mrs. Bellingham, and the two ladies were left to have a cozy gossip and dissect a few characters together, while Lucia and Toby wandered off down one of the long walks.

It didn't take Lucia long to become aware of a certain restraint in Toby's manner. She found his glance frequently coming to rest upon her in a most disconcerting way. Finally she could stand it no longer. When they came upon one of the many little ornamental temples, she pulled him inside, noting his obvious reluctance.

She turned to face him with an air of mock tragedy. "Come now, I beg you, Toby, tell me the worst! I have perhaps developed some dreadful blemish and you are wondering how to break the news to me?"

"Certainly not, m'dear. You are as lovely as ever."

Toby shuffled, ill at ease, and Lucia was just a little exasperated.

"Then why, dear Toby, have you been staring at me this hour past, as though I had two heads?"

"Oh Lord, Lucia, I'm sorry!" Toby paced about in the confined space, one hand pushing through his carefully arranged locks. "The thing is ... well, it never occurred to me that you might misunderstand ... wouldn't have you hurt for the world, but ..." He was floundering, and Lucia, suddenly seeing daylight, strove to keep a straight face.

"Toby dear," she said gently, "I am not expecting you to offer for me. I cannot imagine where you got such an idea, but it is quite nonsensical. I love you dearly, but as a brother only."

His relief was so comical that Lucia could restrain her mirth no longer.

"Oh dear! Your face! You should just see your face!"

He grinned. "I was devilish worried, I don't mind telling you. I mean, I think the world of you, m'dear; you know that, but ... well, the plain fact is, I just ain't cut out for marriage. Can't say I would ever have given it a thought, but for something Hugo said."

"I might have known your wretched cousin would be at the back of it!"

"Oh, it was just a bit of fun. No harm done, eh?"

"No thanks to him!"

"I know you don't like Hugo above half, but he's a capital fellow. I owe him a great deal."

"Hm!" Lucia was skeptical.

"No, truly!" Toby insisted. "It ain't easy to speak of the past, even now, but ... well, d'ye see, my father was a gambler; oh, not just gaming—a real obsession it was. He'd bet on anything—two flies crawling up a wall, anything at all!" His eyes clouded.

"Toby dear, you don't have to tell me."

He continued as though she hadn't spoken. "Two years ago he shot himself." He heard her swift intake of breath. "Seems he'd gambled away everything. There was no entail, and everything had gone— house, lands, the lot. There was nothing left but a mountain of debts."

"Oh Toby!"

He gave her a bleak stare. "It was pretty grim. Fact is, I don't know how I'd have got through without Hugo. He sorted it all out ... paid off the debts ... wouldn't hear a word of objection, though Lord knows, he'd had enough troubles. All in the family, he said ... his mama and mine were sisters, d'ye see?"

"And your mama?"

"Oh, she'd passed away some years before. No— there was only me. Hugo was all for taking me into his household, but I wasn't going to sponge off him for the rest of my days. I decided that the army was the thing for me." He grinned suddenly. "Even then, I couldn't prevent his purchasing a captaincy in the 95th. So you see, my dear, why I won't ever hear a word against Hugo."

"Lord Mandersely certainly seems to have behaved with great generosity," Lucia conceded. "But I still think it very shabby of him to tease you so, and I shall tell him as much when I see him."

She was very quiet on the drive home until she was gently rapped over the knuckles by Lady Springhope's fan.

"Pay attention, child!"

Lucia started. "Forgive me, ma'am. I was a mile away."

"Yes, well, I was saying that Serena Bellingham is holding a musical soirée this day week." She beamed. "You must have a new dress. I have quite made up my mind, so do not be trying to argue. Palest yellow, I think."

When the evening of the party arrived, Lucia was glad of the new dress, for it gave her confidence. She had been to one or two very informal evenings, but she had always had Toby to bear her company. This time he was away.

The pale lemon crêpe was very becoming, edged around the neck with tiny green flowers and caught under the bosom with soft green floating ribbons. Chloe had become expert at arranging Lucia's hair. Tonight it was taken off her face and encouraged to fall in soft ringlets. So it was an entirely charming picture she presented for inspection when they were ready to leave, her green eyes sparkling against the my pallor of her face.

"Quite lovely!" Lady Springhope sighed. "I can scarcely wait for the autumn, dear. Hetty is as dark as you are fair. Between you, you should have every beau for miles around at your feet."

She smoothed down her own plump little figure,

and her eye gleamed wickedly. "Bella Carew will be pea-green with envy. Her Clara is such a plain, whey-faced little creature—hideously spoiled. No one has come anywhere near offering for her all season, and I cannot imagine anyone ever doing so! I declare I could laugh when I think how monstrous unkind she was about my Maria." By which Lucia concluded that Lady Isabel Carew was not her most favorite person.

Mrs. Bellingham welcomed them effusively. "We are looking to you young things to entertain us, so I hope you have come prepared," she twinkled. "And if you should be wishing to dance a little later, my companion, Miss Simms, will happily play for you."

Lucia was introduced to Mrs. Bellingham's daughter Felicity, a friendly girl about her own age, with a pert nose and a quantity of glossy brown curls, and her brother Tom, who was a year or so older and rather serious.

Glancing up, Lucia saw a familiar figure near the door of the card room. "I didn't know Lord Mandersely was to be here," she whispered.

Felicity followed her gaze. "I know Mama invited him, but she had little hope of his accepting, for he seldom ever goes to parties." Her eyes lit with mischief. "Ah, the notorious widow is with him! Have you met her? Countess de Treves . . . they are inseparable these days."

Lucia was intrigued to see the kind of woman that Hugo found irresistible. She was indeed beautiful—tall and willowy, with the kind of style that made every other woman in the room seem frumpish by comparison.

"Mama says Lord Mandersely will probably marry her one of these days, for they are already ... well, you know ..." She giggled. "And he must marry soon, for he is quite old. And of course he *is* terribly rich and she is supposed to be fearfully extravagant."

At that moment the marquis looked across the room. He inclined his head slightly but made no attempt to seek her company, and presently disappeared into the card room.

Lucia found she was enjoying the evening very much, and the entertainment was in full swing when, without warning, Mrs. Bellingham gushed, "And now, Miss Mannering, will you not give us a song? Lady Springhope has been telling me how charmingly you sing."

Lucia was thrown into confusion. She had never sung in public, though she had learned a great number of songs from her mama and often played and sang for her own pleasure. At length, not wishing to appear churlish, she rose and walked to the pianoforte.

"We have a quantity of music, I believe," said Mrs. Bellingham kindly. "Do you wish Miss Simms to play for you?"

"Thank you, ma'am," said Lucia shyly. "I think I can play from memory."

She was aware that Lord Mandersely had come back and was standing quite near her, leaning against the wall, his arms folded across his chest, his profile enigmatic. She began to sing in a hauntingly

71

beautiful voice, and at once became totally absorbed in the music. Accustomed all her life to her mother's greatness, she was genuinely unaware of her own talent. She sang because she loved to sing, and had been brought up in an atmosphere where it was second nature to do so.

The rapturous applause that greeted the end of her performance came as a complete surprise. There were enthusiastic cries for more, and Lucia felt a glow of pride and pleasure. She was searching in her mind for a suitable encore when a hard, carrying voice penetrated the gentle hum of conversation. It came from a thin-faced woman she knew to be Lady Isabel Carew, Lady Springhope's archenemy.

". . . Of course it is no more than one would expect . . . her mother was in the opera, you know. There was a most dreadful scandal. . . ."

In the shocked silence, Lucia sat as though turned to stone. Scarcely conscious of her actions, she scattered a pile of sheet music to the floor and knelt to retrieve it amid a buzz of speculative comment.

Someone was kneeling beside her; a familiar lazy voice murmured in her ear, "Do not let that woman trouble you, Miss Mannering. It is no more than petty jealousy. Her daughter has a voice like a corncrake's."

Through her tears Lucia implored him. "Please, my lord! Help me! Everybody must have heard. I cannot possibly sing again!"

"Nonsense!" His fingers closed around her wrist. "Where is that fighting spirit? Or are you ashamed of your mama now that you are gone up in the world?"

Lucia snatched her hand away and quickly gathered up the rest of the music. Hugo calmly took it from her and returned it to its pile before resuming his place. She straightened up, her eyes unnaturally bright. In a clear voice she apologized to the waiting company, who greeted her words with a sprinkling of sympathetic applause.

Without stopping to think, she sat down and launched into a spirited rendering of a short and extremely idiomatic French song, which caused great shouts of laughter among those with sufficient command of the language to appreciate it.

On the final chord, she glared defiantly at the marquis and rose, to deafening cheers, resolutely refusing the demands for more.

She walked to the window to cool her cheeks, and knew that he had followed her.

"Bravo, Miss Mannering!" He drawled laconically, "I could not have wished for better!"

Her eyes widened in accusation. "Why ... I believe you provoked me quite deliberately!"

"But of course! Only consider ... if I had been sympathetic, you would without a doubt have burst into a flood of tears and made a great spectacle of yourself."

Lucia was forced to admit the truth of what he said, and capitulated with a smile.

"A word of advice, Miss Mannering. Always face up to your adversaries—they cannot then stab you in the back."

"Oh, when it comes to stabbing people in the back, my lord, you must speak as an expert," she said with spirit. "Poor Toby is still recovering from the fright you gave him. That was very shabbily done!"

Hugo put back his head and laughed aloud. "Perhaps ... but quite irresistible at the time, I assure you."

A low, husky voice with just a trace of accent broke into their conversation. "Hugo, my dear, do introduce me to our new little songbird!"

Sophia, Countess de Treves, was even more ravishing at close quarters. Her smooth dark hair accentuated a flawless skin; every feature was perfection.

Her violet eyes met Lucia's with cool indulgence. "My dear Miss Mannering, you will outshine us all. Such a lovely voice!"

"Thank you, Countess. But I am sure no one could ever outshine you. Will you excuse me? I believe Lady Springhope is wanting me." Her eyes met Hugo's just briefly. "I thank you, my lord."

The marquis watched her go, a small smile playing about his mouth.

"She's a very pretty child, isn't she?" Sophia observed coolly. "A trifle pert, perhaps, but then, she is very young. And that song, my dear! So vulgar!"

"Gammon!" said Hugo abruptly. "It was extremely witty!"

The countess was disconcerted, but only for a moment. "Oh well, you men certainly enjoyed it," she said sweetly. "But I do think someone should have a quiet word with her—your aunt, perhaps? Risqué songs may perchance be condoned on the ground of innocent high spirits, but dallying with a man of Sir Gideon Benedict's reputation I feel can do her nothing but harm."

"Benedict?" Hugo frowned. "No, you must be mistaken!"

Sophia's light laugh tinkled out. "I assure you, my dear Hugo, I saw her with my own eyes, not two weeks since, in Piccadilly. I did not then know who she was, of course, but one cannot mistake that coloring. They seemed rather well-acquainted."

Sophia said nothing further, well satisfied that her barbs had gone home. Having been thankfully delivered from the boring old Austrian count whom she had married in his dotage in the mistaken belief that his purse was longer than it had since proved, she had not the slightest intention of losing a prize such as Mandersely to any dewy-eyed little upstart.

After a few moments she suggested casually that they might leave, and Hugo agreed.

Lucia saw them take their leave of Mrs. Bellingham and stop to speak with Lady Springhope, who was still seething over Bella Carew's deliberate slighting of her protégée.

As they turned to go, Lucia lifted her head to smile across at the marquis. The coldness of his nod left her completely bewildered and for some reason absurdly disappointed.

◆ Chapter 5 ◆

The long-awaited letter from her grandfather had come. Her hand trembled as she reread the few curt words: "Granddaughter, I shall expect you at Willow Park on the first day of July." It was signed simply "Rupert Mannering."

Lucia sank despondently into a chair. She found herself swallowing a horrid lump in her throat. Even an effusive note from her Aunt Addie did nothing to raise her spirits.

Lady Springhope was reading her own missive with the aid of an ornate eyeglass, to the accompaniment of many grunts. "Well, child," she said at last. "At all events, he hasn't turned you down flat."

"No, ma'am."

Lady Springhope noted the abject misery in the young face. "It will be all right, m'dear, you'll see."

Lucia burst out passionately, "I don't think I can go through with it." She thrust the note into Lady Springhope's hands. "See! Not one word of encouragement!"

"Oh stuff!" scoffed her ladyship. "That's just Rupert doing a bit of saber rattling! You'll win him over in no time. But we shall have to stir ourselves.

So many things to be done, and only a week to do them."

She scanned her letter again. "Rupert says you are to travel post and charge it up to him, but I won't hear of it. A poor thing it would be, I'm sure, to be hiring coaches when I have a perfectly good one here doing nothing! No, my dear, Newbury shall drive you down to Culliford Cross. He will enjoy the outing, I daresay, for I fear he has been finding his life very dull of late. Oh, and I must send word to Hugo. He will have to escort you."

"Is that necessary?" asked Lucia quickly.

"Yes it is, child. I know everyone assures me the roads are perfectly safe these days, but not a month since, Sir John Carruthers was set upon by footpads on the heath. It was a nasty business, and would have been worse if Lizzie Carruthers had not had a fit of the screaming hysterics and frightened them off!"

Lucia managed a faint smile. "I cannot guarantee to have a fit of hysterics ma'am, but I'm sure we don't need to trouble Lord Mandersely."

"Well, we can't rely on Toby's being here, for the army is demanding much more of his time these days, and even with a groom up on the box with Newbury, I should not be easy. No, it must be Hugo."

Lucia was out shopping when Lord Mandersely called in answer to his aunt's summons. Lady Springhope said he was quite agreeable to the arrangement, a statement which Lucia seriously doubted.

She told him as much when he arrived on the morning of her departure.

There was much coming and going with trunks and bandboxes as he strode into the hall, his riding coat flapping wetly around his legs.

"An inclement day for your journey, Miss Mannering, I wish I could have arranged better for you."

She gave him a wan smile. "And I wish, sir, that you had not been put to the trouble of accompanying me. I cannot think it necessary, especially on such a day."

"It is no trouble." A brooding frown clouded his face. She presented a charming study in a close-fitting silk pelisse of a green that exactly matched her eyes. A delightfully becoming bonnet of the same shade framed her face.

"Miss Mannering," he said abruptly. "A word with you, if you please, before we leave. It will take only a moment. I had hoped to see you last week when I called."

Lucia considered him, half-teasing. "Well, sir, what have I done this time?"

"In private, if you please." He held open the library door.

She hesitated, her lower lip caught provocatively between her teeth, wondering what might happen if she refused . . . and met the answer in his eyes.

She tossed her head and swept past him into the room. The door closed quietly behind her.

The marquis did not speak immediately, but crossed to the window and stood tapping his riding crop upon the window ledge.

"Obviously I am in your black books again," Lucia declared. "Though I am at a loss to know the cause."

"It has come to my attention that you are acquainted—well-acquainted—with Sir Gideon Benedict. I confess I find this hard to believe."

She sighed. "Who told you, my lord? Toby?"

"Toby? No, certainly not! I had it from another source. So! It is true?"

"If it is," she retorted unwisely, "I do not see that it is any concern of yours."

Hugo strode forward and grasped her arm. "You are mistaken, madam! Anything you do is my concern, if I choose to make it so. When I assumed responsibility for you, much against my better judgment, it was at your insistence—or had you forgotten?"

Lucia tried to wrest her arm away, but was held fast. "Oh! How like you to drag that up!" she cried. "Do you know something, my lord marquis? You are a most intolerant man! At the first hint of opposition, you fly into a rage! It would not occur to you that I might find Sir Gideon a loathsome and embarrassing reminder of the past. Oh no! You at once leap to the worst possible conclusion!"

He loosed her arm abruptly and stared. "Intolerant! I! Is that really how I appear to you?"

She shrugged. "I daresay you are not to be blamed, my lord. You are probably not even aware of it, for you will have always been used to having your orders obeyed without question."

The marquis was not used to being patronized, least of all by a slip of a girl with eyes like deep green pools and a disconcertingly direct manner. After the initial shock, he found the experience diverting. "I cannot imagine you ever obeying anyone without question."

She gave the idea her full consideration. "I might. It would depend upon the circumstances."

Hugo held up a hand. "Very well, in future I will try to be more conciliatory, but on one point I am adamant. You will have no further dealings with Benedict." He met her limpid gaze. "Oh, come now, Miss Mannering ... you don't even like the man! You have just admitted as much. And I am not only thinking of your good; Hetty will be here in a few weeks' time, and God knows, she's capable of embroiling herself in enough mischief without letting anyone like Benedict into her orbit." He paused. "So—do I have your word on it?"

Lucia inclined her head. "Certainly, my lord," she said demurely. "You will find I am always open to reasoned argument."

He threw back his head and laughed. "I think it is as well that you are going away for a while, Miss Mannering."

As the marquis held open the door for her, he put a staying hand on her shoulder. "You are not really troubled about meeting your grandfather?"

She nodded.

"There is nothing to fear." Hugo's voice was surprisingly gentle. "He cannot fail to be enchanted."

Lucia looked up, her heart beating fast as their eyes met.

He seemed suddenly to recollect himself. His

manner became brusque. "I think we should leave, if you are ready."

"Yes, of course—if I may just run up and bid good-bye to Lady Springhope. I shall not keep you above a moment."

Chloe was enjoying herself hugely. She hugged around her the new blue cloak, a present from her ladyship. Never in her wildest imaginings had she ever thought to ride in such a grand vehicle. When she was brought up from the country by her uncle to be put into service, she had ridden on the stage. But then she had been squashed between a fat, evil-smelling woman, whose several chins wobbled with every movement of the lumbering coach, and a man with bony elbows that prodded her ribs until she was black and blue.

It didn't begin to compare with the elegance of her ladyship's traveling chaise, with its crimson padded cushions. Chloe thought that it had been a very good day's work for them both when Miss Lucia had run away from Bruton Street. Not that she was looking any too chirpy at the moment, but perhaps it was the weather making her miserable.

But Lucia was hardly aware of the weather. She stared blindly out of the window as they rolled through Knightsbridge and Hammersmith. The rain, which had almost stopped, began to spot heavily again as the sky darkened. Thunder rumbled ominously in the distance, and Chloe stirred uneasily.

"Ooh, miss! There's going to be a storm! Suppose the horses bolt?"

"Don't be silly," Lucia snapped absently.

"Newbury would not permit them to bolt. Neither would Lord Mandersely."

A sudden blinding flash of lightning slashed the sky, followed at once by a terrifying crash of thunder. Chloe screamed. Even Lucia felt a twinge of unease as the dose was repeated. Then the rain came, lashing down on the roof of the coach, drowning out all other sound. She could feel the horses straining jerkily at the bit.

Hugo's figure loomed up at the window, rain streaming from the rim of his beaver hat. His black stallion was reined in tight, its eyes rolling wildly.

"All right?" he shouted.

She nodded.

"We're nearing Hounslow. There's a small inn up ahead ... we'll take shelter there until the storm abates."

He vanished from view as thunder again shattered the air. The frightened horses hurtled forward until at last they swerved off the road and came to a plunging halt. Lucia peered through the rain-drenched windows at a scene of utter pandemonium; gigs, curricles, phaetons, any number of assorted vehicles packed the cobbled yard, and hostlers scurried back and forth, bent double by the rain.

The door of the coach was wrenched open and Lord Mandersely held out his arms. "Come, quickly!" He swung her across the muddy ground, depositing her firmly on the doorstep of the inn.

"It is not where I would have chosen to stop; there is a main about to start in the barn at the rear." She looked blank. "Cockfighting. The place is crammed to the ceiling, but the landlord is putting a small parlor on the first floor at our disposal and will bring us some hot coffee." He turned. "Where's that girl of yours?"

Chloe was still huddled in her corner, sobbing hysterically, convinced that the end of the world had come. When shouting produced no results, Lord Mandersely heaved himself into the coach and slapped her sharply across the face.

"Stop at once! Look to your mistress!" She gaped at him wild-eyed and scrambled down the steps and across the muddy yard.

Lucia put a soothing arm about her and led her toward the stair.

In the swell of voices about them, one stood out and she spun around, her heart missing a beat.

Sir Gideon was lounging in the archway leading to the public bar. He strolled over, and his arm across the banister rail barred their path. Her grip on Chloe tightened.

"Lucia! We have a happy knack, do we not, of meeting unexpectedly?" His eyes flicked over her. "And to think, 'twas a bird of a very different plumage that brought me here. Where is the faithful Toby? You are surely not alone?" His expression altered abruptly; Lord Mandersely was in the doorway, shaking the rain from his hat. "Ah! I see the watchdog has given up his place to the master!"

The sight of Hugo broke the spell for Lucia. She said coldly, "Lord Mandersely is escorting me to my grandfather's."

"I see!"

Hugo came swiftly across, his brow thunderous. Sir Gideon stood back and with a mocking bow indicated the stairs. Lucia urged Chloe forward, and heard Hugo's clipped tones: "Have a care, Benedict—you live dangerously!"

Sir Gideon laughed, and Lucia heard no more, for they were being ushered into a bright parlor, where a few weak flames struggled for life in the big stone fireplace.

Hugo followed them in almost at once, a serving wench close at his heels with a steaming coffeepot. The coffee was drunk for the most part in silence, which neither seemed inclined to break. Though no reference was made to Benedict's presence, it lay heavily between them.

Hugo crossed to the window. "The storm appears to have passed, Miss Mannering," he said curtly. "I think we may safely proceed."

"Yes, of course." Lucia hastily gathered her gloves and reticule. She stole a glance at his face. "My lord ...? I could not avoid Sir Gideon. ..."

His expression softened slightly. "I know. I am only sorry I was not here. Newbury had trouble with the horses."

There was no sign of Sir Gideon as they left. The inn was almost deserted, but from the barn at the rear came the sounds of shouting and chanting.

The sun broke through with dazzling brilliance as they crossed the heath, that dreaded stretch of moorland so feared by Lady Springhope, and they encountered nothing more fearsome than an occasional jackrabbit. They turned onto the Bath road, and all too soon came to Culliford Cross. The coach halted before the entrance to a curving driveway, and Lord Mandersely rode up..

"You have arrived, Miss Mannering."

Her heart began to flutter uncomfortably. "Will you not come in with me, sir? I am sure my grandfather would wish to thank you."

"I think not, Miss Mannering. Your reconciliation will be better achieved without the presence of an outsider."

He looked at her for a moment and then smiled. "Chin up, little spitfire! I hope all goes well for you." With a final salute he wheeled the big stallion and thundered away.

Once out of sight, Hugo slowed the animal to a trot and fell to contemplating the memory of Lucia Mannering's face—pale and tense, the green eyes large and overbright, with just the suspicion of a tremble about that stubborn chin.

He should have gone with her, helped her over the initial ordeal. Irritably he spurred Rufus to a gallop. The sky had again turned a sickly yellow and was darkening by the minute. There was an eerie stillness, and over to the west, thunder rumbled constantly.

He decided to make once more for the inn, before the heavens opened. The heath was deserted. Nothing moved, even the smallest creature had gone scurrying to earth; silent birds huddled in the trees. As he rounded a particularly thick clump of trees, three men rode out and barred his way. All carried pistols and were masked.

Hugo dragged hard on the rein and brought the stallion to a halt. He surveyed the trio calmly. "If you are hoping for money or valuables, my friends, your luck is quite out. I am carrying very little on me."

"Stow it!" growled the leading felon. A hasty conference ensued.

"What d'ye think, Charlie? Is this the right cove?"

" 'E's a flash cull, right enough."

"Nag fits an' all ... black stallion's what 'e said. 'Ere, stow yer daddles!" snapped Charlie, as Hugo took one hand off the rein.

"I beg your pardon!" his lordship apologized. He sat back wearily. "Gentlemen, you appear to be somewhat at a loss! Would it expedite matters at all if I were to tell you that I am Mandersely?"

They stared.

"Cor! You're a cool one!" The first man scratched under his hat brim with the barrel of his pistol. "A very cool cove, you are! Well, lads—best get it over."

Hugo's keen ears picked up, above the constant rumble of thunder, hoofbeats approaching very fast; someone was trying to beat the weather, no doubt. At the same moment, his assailants also heard, and were thrown into temporary confusion.

Hugo seized his chance. Dropping his hand to his pocket, he fired his pistol through his coat at the man on the right and heard the man's yell of pain as he fell. Almost simultaneously he dug his knees in hard and drove the horse straight between the two other riders, who were so unnerved by the sight of their intended victim coming at them like the wrath of God that they panicked and discharged their pistols harmlessly into the air.

Hugo passed between them, let go the reins for a split-second, and pushed outward with both hands, unseating them to the accompaniment of loud curses. He didn't wait, but pounded onward. He heard a shout, and a rider drew level.

"That was spendidly done," the man shouted. "Sorry I wasn't a few seconds sooner."

Hugo flashed him a wide grin. "You provided the necessary diversion, my friend. My thanks!" Finding they were not followed, they slackened pace.

"Whew!" The man laughingly drew breath. "I'm glad to have been of some service, my lord."

"You know me?" Hugo's glance met a pair of humorous gray eyes.

"My lord, who in the fashionable world does not know and try to ape Lord Mandersely? To own a pair of hessians with Mandersely tassels . . . to achieve with one's neckcloth a Mandersely fall ... or learn the art of raising a quizzing glass just so!"

Hugo put up a hand. "Enough!" he begged. He eyed the stranger's stocky figure, the riding coat with its one modest cape. "I would never have taken you for one of the *beau monde*, sir," he observed in a droll voice.

"And you would be right," the young man grinned. "However, I *do* have a young brother, and he assures me you are all the crack." He stretched a hand across the saddle. "My name is Conrad, my lord, Charles Conrad."

The storm was threatening again, and the first

large spots of rain splashed down. "Make for the inn," shouted Hugo above a clap of thunder. They broke into a gallop as the drops suddenly increased to a deluge.

"I was going there anyway, my lord. That same young rip of a brother has sloped off to a cockfight—he has a friend with a likely bird—and Mama, getting wind of the affair, must believe him to be in mortal danger from bad company. I am sent to fetch the miscreant home."

The lashing rain and the danger from wildly whipping branches prevented any further conversation until they reached their destination.

The horses stabled, they made a dash for the barn. The steamy atmosphere was choked with sluggishly swirling feathers. From the pit, tier upon tier of benches rose into the rafters, supporting a rowdy, clamoring mob of mostly young bloods. Hugo and Charles Conrad pushed their way past young Corinthians hotly disputing form, and were in time to witness the dying throes of the final contest.

Hugo's eye traveled slowly along the front ranks of spectators until it came to rest on the figure he was seeking. Leaning forward, his features a distorted mask of vicious sensuality, Sir Gideon Benedict sat, totally absorbed in the macabre spectacle being enacted before him.

A red cock, a magnificent bird, strong and arrogant, strutted around the pit emitting a harsh, triumphant cry, while a smaller dun cock slumped dejectedly in the center of the arena. A spur had al ready pierced its lung, and blood was slowly choking it.

"By God! The dun's rattled!" The cry was taken up and echoed around the huge barn.

As though playing to the gallery, the dying bird suddenly lurched across the sod and grappled its adversary. Like pugilists they shuffled around the pit, until with a supreme effort the dun pulled away and jerked erect; once, twice, three times it leaped with deadly grace and gaffed the red cock. Its cry of victory was drowned as the blood gushed from its throat, and the two birds pitched forward simultaneously, dead.

A cheer rose into the rafters, and the spectators at once began to elbow their way out, intent upon reaching the inn, where they could debate the finer points of the contest in comfort. Sir Gideon sat on in tight-lipped fury; it would seem he had lost a valuable bird.

"Well, my lord," said Charles. "That would appear to be that." A young fop in the full glory of yellow pantaloons, green coat, and vividly striped waistcoat, topped by a monstrous sweep of a cravat, pushed toward them.

"Ho there, Charles! I didn't know you were here. What capital sport, eh?" Jason Conrad became aware of his brother's companion. "I say! Lord Mandersely! Charles . . . you never said you were acquainted with Lord Mandersely."

"Mind your manners, puppy!" reproved his brother. "I apologize for the lad's shortcomings, my lord. As you can see, he is scarcely out of leading reins."

"Come off it, Charles! This is the greatest thing ever!"

Hugo watched this touching family reunion with lazy amusement. Occasionally his eyes lifted to scan the crowd.

Jason watched his every move. Hugo put up his glass; his brows arched delicately. "Is this the young buck who aspires to be my rival?"

"By jove, I could never be that!" Jason enthused, quite unabashed. "But now that I know you, I shall not feel in the least shy about asking your advice, my lord. . . . I must find Bertram . . . he'll be green, I can tell you. . . ."

"Sometimes he makes me feel positively old," observed his brother whimsically. "I hope he did not annoy you, sir?"

There was no reply, and he turned to find his lordship's gaze riveted with a curious intentness upon a large redhaired gentleman. At that moment the man also saw Hugo, and Charles surprised a look of such malevolence that it was almost unnerving. The look was instantly masked, and the man came forward with every appearance of civility, so that Charles began to feel that he must have imagined the whole thing.

"Mandersely! Now, here's a strange thing—that we should be meeting twice in the same day."

Hugo was urbane. "You were not, perhaps, expecting to see me again?"

The Irishman flushed a dull red. "You appear to have had an accident with your coat, my lord."

Hugo contemplated the hole in his pocket and carefully rubbed the charred edges between slim fingers.

"It is nothing, my dear Benedict. A trifling accident ... some vermin I encountered on the heath. I was forced to ... er, deal with them."

Sir Gideon's smile had grown sickly. "You must take care, Marquis—vermin can strike when one least expects. And now, if you will excuse me, I have an appointment."

Charles Conrad was baffled by this exchange.

"I think that gentleman does not like you, my lord," he said quietly.

"How very acute of you, Conrad." Hugo's voice was quite without expression, and Charles, glancing at him, decided that further comment would be unwise.

They walked on in silence. The crowd had dispersed, and the rain had stopped. As they approached the inn, two limping figures came into view. They were making furtively for the back door, supporting a third, inert form.

"My lord!" Charles gripped Hugo's arm. "There go your assailants. ... I'd bet money on it!"

Hugo watched until they were out of sight and then walked on.

"But ... surely you are going to accost them. Bring the creatures to book?"

"I think not."

"But ... my lord ..."

"You see, my friend, I feel they are already going to be in enough trouble over the appalling way they bungled their task."

Conrad stopped dead in his tracks. "But damnit, that means you think what happened back there was not just a casual holdup?"

Hugo smiled grimly. "*I know*," he said softly, "that our inept trio was sent quite deliberately to kill me!"

◆ Chapter 6 ◆

Lucia watched Lord Mandersely's retreating figure with an inexplicable sense of abandonment and loss.

Then the coach was turning in through the big iron gates, and he was lost to view. They were riding sedately up a curving, tree-lined driveway, and she roused herself to lean forward, eager for a first glimpse of the house; suddenly it was there—a long, sprawling building of mellow brick. Thunder still rumbled, but a sudden blinding shaft of sunlight burst through the clouds, setting the mullioned windows ablaze in welcome.

Before the coach had rolled to a halt, the front doors were flung open and a thin, wispy woman of indeterminate age came hurrying down the steps, picking up her blue dimity skirts. Lucia stepped swiftly down and was instantly enveloped in this good lady's embrace.

"My dear, dear niece ... Oh! What a day this is! How I have longed ... have hoped ..."

"Aunt Addie?"

"Oh! ... Yes, of course, dear child, how silly of me! I am just so excited...." She stood back, holding Lucia's hands as though fearing she might vanish again at any moment. Her pale blue eyes were bright with tears as she gazed at last on her brother's child. "It is unbelievable—the likeness! Aurelia did mention it in her letter, but I never dreamed . . . I don't know how Papa will take it I'm sure, but never mind, you are here. Come along in. Bassett will attend to your maid and see your boxes taken up."

A portly old man had followed her down the steps. "Bassett, isn't this a wonderful day?"

The old man had served the family all his life. "It is indeed, Miss Addie, ma'am." He bowed with quiet deference. "May I say, miss, how happy we are to have Mr. Freddie's daughter under our own roof at last."

"Why, thank you, Bassett!" Lucia was touched by his obvious sincerity.

She followed her aunt into the cool spacious hall, hardly hearing her continuous prattle. This is where my father was born. . . . She felt a sudden thrill of belonging. He must have run across this hall a hundred times, climbed the staircase, his hand holding this very rail. To Lucia, who had never known a settled home, it was a strange and magical experience.

"Papa insisted that he must see you the instant you arrived," her aunt was saying. "I told him you would be quite done up after your journey, but he is so difficult . . . She looked vague. "Of course, you mustn't scruple to say if you should want to rest."

Lucia smiled reassuringly. "Dear aunt, I am not in the least fagged. If I could just wash off a little of the grime and make myself tidy, I shall be quite ready to present myself." This wasn't strictly true, but she decided there was no point in putting off the dreaded moment.

Aunt Addie looked relieved. "He has been very ill, you know, and is indeed still far from well. Dr. Weston advises that he must not get overexcited, but he will fly into a miff at the least setback, so if you could try not to upset him . . ."

Lucia stifled a slight twinge of irritation, as her aunt threw open the door of a large airy bedchamber, attractively hung in floral prints.

"What a charming room!" Lucia exclaimed in delight.

"It is pretty, isn't it?" Aunt Addie sighed wistfully. "It has been so seldom used, but now you are come, all that is at an end."

Lucia removed her bonnet and pelisse and smoothed down the cream-spotted muslin. She would have preferred to change her dress for a fresh one after sitting in it for so long, but her aunt was hopping about like an agitated hen, so she quickly washed and tidied her hair.

"There, I am ready," she said, displaying a totally false air of confidence.

By the time her aunt was scratching on the panel of the library door, her stomach was in a miserable knot. A curt voice ordered them to enter, and Aunt Addie was twittering, "Here is Lucia, come at last, Papa!"

Lucia had a fleeting impression of heavy crimson hangings and a quantity of oak wainscoting, before her eye was caught and held, with a heart-stopping jolt, by the oil painting over the fireplace. The gown was of an earlier age, the hair more elaborately dressed, but in every other respect she was looking at herself!

From the depths of an enormous armchair near the fireplace an irascible voice demanded her attention.

"Well, come nearer, girl! I can't see you if you stand over there by the door! That fool of a doctor forbids me to rise, and I have no intention of craning my neck."

Lucia dragged her eyes from the portrait and met her aunt's troubled gaze.

An ebony cane rapped impatiently on the floor, and Lucia walked slowly forward.

She had hoped for some resemblance to her father, but there was none. Colonel Rupert Mannering was a striking figure of a man in spite of the ravages left by illness. Bushy eyebrows above keen dark eyes and a large hooked nose gave his face a kind of fierce strength. Pure white hair sprang vigorously from a wide forehead. He wore it unfashionably long, tied back in a queue. Only the unnatural parchment color of the skin betrayed his frailty.

Lucia stood gravely before him, seeing the intense shock in his eyes. The skin was stretched tight across his cheekbones, and one thin, blue-veined hand shook as it plucked querulously at the fur rug across his knees. The tension became unbearable. At last his harsh staccato voice broke the silence.

"So . . . you are my granddaughter?"

She let out her breath on a sigh. "Yes, sir, I am Lucia."

"I will have no fancy foreign names in this house. As long as you remain here you will be Lucy."

Indignation flared, but she controlled it almost at once. "Very well, sir," she agreed quietly. "If that is what you wish."

"It is! And one other stipulation." He glared under lowered brows. "I will not have my son's name—or that woman's—mentioned in my presence. No doubt your aunt will be only too happy to indulge in foolish reminiscence, but I will have none of it. Is that clear?"

Scalding tears of rage and disappointment were threatening to blind her; angry words rose to her lips, but frantic pleading signs from her aunt made her swallow the lump in her throat and jerk her head in silent agreement.

"Then you may go." He dismissed her without another word.

"I won't stay!" Lucia stormed, as Aunt Addie hurried her away from the library and into a small cozy parlor. "Did you hear what he called my mother? How dare he! I should never have let myself be talked into coming."

"Oh, don't say that, dear." Tears were coursing down her aunt's thin cheeks. She collapsed onto a sofa, her cap askew, and fumbled for her handkerchief. "He didn't mean it, I'm sure. He was very upset ... I feared he would be, the moment I saw you ... so like dear Mama. Oh, do give him time, my dear." She dabbed ineffectually at her reddened eyes. "I do *so* want you to stay!"

Lucia instantly flew across the room and flung a

comforting arm around the older woman's shoulders. "Oh, don't cry, dear aunt. Of course I must stay. Good gracious, I have already put everyone to a vast amount of trouble on my account! A fine thing it would be if I cried off at the first setback!"

She smiled shakily. "You mustn't mind my temper. I have often been rebuked for it, but it never lasts."

But in spite of her determination to rise above this bad beginning, and in spite of her aunt's constant efforts to make her feel at home, Lucia was desperately lonely at first. She longed for Toby's uncomplicated camaraderie and often sought solace in the peace of the gardens. There were willows everywhere, drooping their graceful fronds, whispering to her gently as she passed. On hot days she spent hours in their shade, daydreaming.

When she was exploring the house one day, she found a music room tucked away at the far end—a sort of garden room.

"Goodness!" Aunt Addie exclaimed, when Lucia begged permission to use it. "of course you may use it, child. Lud, it has scarcely been used since Freddie left."

She was always eager to talk of Freddie, the dear companion of her childhood. In the nursery, Freddie's toy soldiers were still laid neatly in their boxes, side by side with her dolls.

"I have always hoped that someday this room would be used again." She sighed. "I spend a lot of time keeping everything just so."

Lucia felt desperately sorry for her. She was a simple, silly creature, and she must have led a very lonely life all these years, shut up here with her father.

Lady Springhope had said Grandfather found her a trial, and Lucia could quite see this, for even she found her irritating at times, but she was unfailingly kind, and so embarrassingly proud of her newfound niece that Lucia felt herself to be disloyal even to think it.

Her grandfather had made no further attempt to communicate with her. He had taken to his bed on the evening of her arrival, and although the doctor could find no worsening in his condition, he declared himself unfit to rise.

By the middle of the second week Lucia decided that the time had come to attempt to break the deadlock. Accordingly, when her aunt announced, as she invariably did, that she must go and give Papa his physic and see if he had any little commissions for her, Lucia said brightly, "Aunt Addie, you are looking tired. I think you should go and lie down. I will attend to Grandfather."

Aunt Addie gasped and turned pale. "B-but you can't . . ."

"Indeed, yes. I am very good in a sickroom."

"He wouldn't stand for it. . . . I beg you, think of the consequences." She saw the determined gleam in her niece's eye and groped for her vinaigrette.

"Dear child, you'll ruin everything. Oh, I don't feel at all well!"

"Then you should certainly go and rest," Lucia said firmly. "And don't worry, dear aunt."

A few moments later Lucia stood outside her grandfather's bedchamber, appalled by her own temerity. But Lady Springhope's words were echoing in her ears: "Don't let Rupert browbeat you!" Well, ignoring her existence amounted to the same thing. She knocked firmly and went in.

It was very much the room of a retired colonel—strictly utilitarian furniture and plain dark green curtains. At one end of the room was a huge four-poster bed, and there, under a green tapestry quilt, banked by a mountain of pillows, Colonel Mannering sat with military erectness, wrapped in a crimson velvet robe.

"You're five minutes late!" he barked. As Lucia closed the door quietly and approached the bed, the beetle brows came together with alarming ferocity. "Who the devil permitted you to come in here?"

She flinched. "No one, sir. But since you are unable to leave your room at present, I took it upon myself to come to you."

"Then damnit, you can take yourself off again and wait until you're sent for. And tell your aunt I wish to see her."

Lucia hoped her voice didn't tremble. "I'm afraid I can't do that, sir. Aunt Addie is lying down. She has a headache."

"Addie always has a headache!" he growled. "Never knew such a woman for having pettifogging ailments."

"Well, I daresay it has been a very trying time for her, your being ill for so long. That is why I suddenly saw how I might help her—by looking after you while she rests." She clasped her hands very tight to stop them shaking.

"Very commendable, I'm sure, but I believe we need not trouble you. You may pull the bell for my man Henry on your way out."

"I am not leaving. I am to give you your physic."

Lucia moved across to the table and poured the prescribed dose. Behind her the colonel was marshaling his resources for a desperate last-ditch stand. "I won't have it! It's rank insubordination!" he roared.

Suddenly Lucia wasn't afraid. He was exactly like a small boy wanting his own way. "Oh, come, sir! I am not one of your cowering soldiers. I am your granddaughter—or had you forgot?" Her eyes were twinkling as she held out the medicine.

His voice dropped almost to a whisper. "No. I cannot forget. Not if I have to look at you."

She sat on the edge of the bed, the glass clasped in her hand. "I know. I had not realized the likeness was quite so marked. It must have been a dreadful shock for you. But when you are more used to the idea, could we not try to be friends?"

He stared at her for a long time, his eyes hard and bright. Then his eyebrows quivered. "Oh, give me the physic, child. I see I shall have no peace if you don't get your way. It was bad enough with only one woman to nag at me. Did your aunt not tell you I was not to be overexcited?"

"Yes, sir . . ." Her voice was hesitant.

"Well?" he barked.

"I think you use it quite shamelessly as a means of

getting your own way,"she ventured. For a moment she thought she had gone too far. His face worked, his nostrils, his mouth opened and shut. Oh God! she thought. He's going to have an attack!

And then suddenly he let our a great shout of laughter. "You are a cheeky malapert! But at least you are no cringing milk-and-water miss." He cuffed her cheek with one hand. "Get along with you, now . . . I want to rest."

Lucia got up slowly. "I haven't tired you?"

"No. I always rest at this time."

"Can I do nothing more? Make your pillows more comfortable perhaps?"

"No, no! I can't abide being messed about!"

"Then I will leave you, sir."

"Lucy?"

She held her breath. It was the first time he had actually addressed her by name. "Yes, sir?"

"You may return later and read to me."

She was smiling as she closed the door.

Later that same week, she was able to write to Lady Springhope:

I now sit with Grandfather regularly, and he gets stronger every day. We have come to understand each other quite well, and I am learning that he is nothing like as fierce as he would have one believe.

He makes no mention of my parents, and I have no wish to endanger the delicate fabric of our relationship by doing so. It is the one small cloud on my horizon.

There are some very pleasant families in the neighborhood. . . .

Lucia particularly liked Mrs. Conrad, a plump amiable lady with a large family. Her eldest son, Charles, came on Tuesdays to pass the evening with her grandfather, and Mrs. Conrad came twice a week to take tea with Aunt Addie and bring her all the latest gossip.

She had greeted Lucia warmly and said with a twinkle, "You will think us very shallow creatures, my dear child, but we are so quiet here, that the most trivial events assume a quite ridiculous importance. I am afraid you are bound to find yourself the center of attention—until something else comes along to distract us."

Lucia laughed. "I shall strive to bear it with fortitude, ma'am."

Mrs. Conrad patted her hand. "Good girl." She selected a comfit from a large dish at her side and nibbled it. "My dear Addie, I must tell you at once . . . Charles has been appointed as second secretary to the lord chancellor! What do you think of that? Mr. Conrad is so proud of him. I am told that to have reached such a position by the age of twenty-eight is something quite out of the common!"

Lucia said warmly, "Your son must be very clever, ma'am."

"Why yes, I believe he is." She helped herself to another comfit. "I could wish Jason was likely to follow him."

"Well, so he may, dear." Aunt Addie beamed encouragement. "He's not much more than a baby."

His mother sighed. "The height of his ambition at present seems centered upon becoming a fashionable beau in the manner of Mr. Brummell or Lord Mandersely."

"Is Lord Mandersely considered a beau?" chuckled Lucia.

"Oh, my dear, if you could hear Jason, you would not doubt it for a moment. Lord Mandersely arrived at some horrid cockfight with Charles the other week, and he actually spoke to Jason. Since then the boy has been impossible to live with."

They laughed, and the conversation drifted on to other things, but Lucia's thoughts lingered with maddening persistence on a dark, intolerant face and a pair of sleepy eyes.

One morning at the beginning of her third week at Willow Park, Aunt Addie sought Lucia out to say that Ned was to drive her into the town, if she should care to come along. She found her niece looking peaky and abstracted. At once she began to fuss. Was she sickening for something? Should Dr. Weston be sent for? She would not dream of leaving her poor angel in such a way. . . .

Lucia bore all this and more in similar vein, until finally her patience snapped. Poor Aunt Addie looked so hurt that she was instantly penitent.

"Please, aunt," she pleaded, "just go off and do your shopping. I promise you I have nothing more than a fit of the blue devils; it will soon pass."

To her relief, Aunt Addie believed her. When she

had gone, Lucia wandered through to the music room. She sat at the pianoforte, staring out at the willow trees, seeing them through a mist of tears. It was absurd and childish, she chided herself, but she was still young enough to mind that it was her nineteenth birthday, and not a soul in all the world knew it!

Lucia longed for her lively, lovely Mama, who had always made birthdays fun. She began to sing a haunting Neapolitan lament that poured out all her misery and all her longings.

As the last notes of the song died away she looked up through her tears to see the colonel standing in the doorway leaning heavily on his ebony stick, staring at her with a fierce, unfathomable expression.

Lucia quickly brushed a hand across her eyes. "Oh, I have disturbed you! I am sorry. I thought you would not hear."

"Well, I did hear," he said gruffly. "You have a very beautiful voice, my child, but no one so young should know unhappiness such as you have just expressed so movingly. For that unhappiness, I fear I am much to blame."

"Oh, Grandfather! If I could just talk to you about them sometimes!"

He stared down into the passionate young face upturned to him, and for a moment his vision blurred and it was Marianne who seemed to stand there, her arms outstretched. Then he blinked rapidly and it was only Lucy, this child who had forced her way into his heart, a heart for so long fettered by bitterness and grief. He held out his free arm and with a sob she flew to him and the arm closed tightly around her. He patted her awkwardly as she clung to him.

"Ah, child ... child! What a curse is pride! So much time—all wasted!"

Lucia looked up, her eyes bright through her tears. "Oh, but we'll make up for it, won't we? It isn't too late!"

For the very first time, she saw him smile. "Let's see if we can make a start," he said. "I had almost forgotten why I came to find you."

Intrigued, she allowed herself to be led back through the house to the front door. At the foot of the front steps, a young groom was walking a beautiful young bay mare. Lucia looked from it to her grandfather.

Colonel Mannering said gruffly, "A birthday present from an old fool who is just beginning to discover what he has been missing all these years."

He gave her a little push, and she ran down the steps to fondle the lovely elegant creature as it nuzzled her hand.

"Oh, but you are beautiful!" she whispered, fondling the soft ears. "Does she have a name?"

"I daresay, but name her what you will."

"Mignonne! For you are such a delicate creature." She cast an impish grin in the colonel's direction. "If Grandfather will permit you a fancy foreign name!"

She ran back up the steps, reaching on tiptoe to kiss his cheek.

"No, now ... enough of that!" he protested, but there was a decided gleam in his eye.

"But I don't understand! How did you know? And how did you guess how much I have always longed for a horse of my own?"

He snorted. "Any child of Freddie's was bound to love horses." His face clouded. "As to your birthday . . ."

He took her hand; slowly and painfully he climbed the stairs, pausing every few steps to rest.

"You should not have come downstairs. You are tiring yourself," she chided.

"Don't fuss, child! You know I can't abide fussing females."

He led the way to his library, where he sank wearily into the leather armchair and picked up the heavy family Bible. On the flyleaf, immediately below her father's name, was her own—Lucia Marianne, July 18, 1789.

The colonel's mind went back over the years. "I could not condone Freddie's behavior . . . I would not forgive! When his letter came, telling me of your birth, I tried to put it from my mind; but my conscience plagued me until it was properly registered. And every year since then, I have remembered you on this day."

Lucia dropped to the floor beside him, her arms resting confidently now upon his knee. "Oh, what a lot of time we have to make up!"

Aunt Addie found them still there upon her return. She was in transports of delight over the birthday, and distressed that she had not known. "For we could have had a celebration!" She brightened. "Perhaps it is not too late—a small informal affair—just one or two friends—the Conrads, and possibly the Mashams. I could send word. Nothing formal, it would be too much to ask of cook, but a small supper party. I believe it might be managed, don't you think so, Papa?"

Colonel Mannering informed her that she may do as she wished—it was his intention to retire to his bed.

When she crept in to see him late in the evening, Lucia thought he was looking tired, but he pooh-poohed the idea. She sat beside him and shyly slid her hand into his. "I just came in to say thank you for a wonderful day."

"So ... you've enjoyed yourself? How was your aunt's party?"

She chuckled. "Oh, I felt very important. It was a nice feeling, but this morning was nicer!"

The soft candlelight played over the bent head, turning it to pure silver. He put up a hand and touched it. It was unbelievably painful learning to love again and knowing he must lose her before long.

"Charles Conrad came to say good-bye. He is returning to London in the next few days." The colonel's voice was abrupt. "He asked if he might call on you in town. D'you like the fellow?"

"Mr. Conrad? Why, yes, he seems very nice."

"He is much taken with you. I suppose you could do a lot worse—he's going a long way, that young man. But there, I imagine you'll have 'em lining up for your favors if Aurelia has any say in it!"

"Oh, really, Grandfather! What nonsense you talk!

I am only interested in one man." She leaned forward and kissed him. "And it's high time he was asleep." She slid off the bed. "Good night, sir, sleep well."

Lucia was enchanted with the little mare, and they were soon a familiar sight in the district. One morning she was within sight of the gates when two riders turned in, one of them in uniform. Visitors for Grandfather, she thought absently.

A moment later there was a great shout, a cocked hat was being waved madly in the air, and Lucia glimpsed a familiar blond head as horse and rider came charging toward her.

"Toby!" They clasped hands, laughing and talking both at once. "Oh Toby, it is good to see you! You are so grand, I thought you were someone important!"

"Baggage!"

She gripped his hand hard. "Oh, but I have missed you, especially at the beginning."

"But not anymore, eh?" He raised an expressive eyebrow. "It's all right, m'dear, anyone with half an eye can see that all goes well with you." What say you, Hugo—don't she positively glow?"

Lord Mandersely had ridden up to join them, viewing their youthful antics with the air of an indulgent uncle. He subjected Lucia to one of his careful appraisals, a slight smile playing about his lips.

She at once became aware of the shabbiness of her old brown riding habit, which she had not worn for more than a twelvemonth, and which had required much judicious alteration before it could be made to fit.

As always, under his scrutiny, her chin lifted and his smile widened. "Miss Mannering, I am delighted to find you looking so much yourself. I infer your visit has been a complete success."

"It took a little time, sir." "But, yes, all is now well."

They all turned and rode slowly back up the drive. At the front steps Hugo dismounted and walked across to Lucia. He held up his hands to lift her down, holding her for just a fraction longer than was necessary.

Flustered, Lucia turned to Toby. "Let me look at you properly." She stood back to admire his distinctive uniform of Rifle green, tracing the frogging with a delicate finger. "Oh yes, you are very grand! Quite irresistible!" She dropped the banter suddenly. "You're going away, aren't you?"

"Friday." He grinned. "Things are on the move in Spain, so we should be seeing some action."

He sounded so like a small boy that she smiled and took his hand. "You must meet Grandfather. He will want to know all about it."

"I am charged with messages from my aunt," said Hugo as they moved into the house, "she is to visit Mama the first week in September, on her way back from Maria's in Gloucestershire. It is her intention to take Hetty back to town with her, and if you are agreeable, she will pick you up en route. It means but a small detour—Mandersely is not above fifteen miles from here."

"That is kind of her."

"But you are not enthusiastic?"

"Isn't it silly? I was so reluctant to come, and now I find I don't in the least wish to leave."

"Not silly at all. It simply means you have come to regard this as your home."

The presence of two such personable young men in the house set Aunt Addie aflutter. They must take some refreshment.... Bassett must fetch the madeira and the best glasses. She hovered, anxious that it should be to their liking. Toby assured her solemnly that it was just as it should be, and Lord Mandersely raised one whimsical eyebrow and devoted himself to the task of putting her aunt at ease. Lucia presently bore them off to her grandfather's room, where she left them to talk.

Walking with Toby in the garden before they left, Lucia found him full of enthusiasm for the colonel.

"I'll tell you something, Lucia—he thinks the world of you. There is such a warmth in his eye when he speaks of you!"

Her whole face softened. "Yes, we have become very close. I shall miss him dreadfully when I leave." She smiled sadly at Toby. "I shall miss you too."

"Stuff! You'll have so many men at your feet, you won't give me a thought." He took her by the shoulders and studied her with unaccustomed seriousness. "If you are ever in any trouble, with that villain Benedict for instance, let Hugo know. He'll see him off!" He saw Lucia's expression and shook her slightly. "Oh, I know you and he don't always deal together—and I'll admit he has a damned disagreeable way with him at times, but there's none better in a fix."

Lucia, however, assured him that it wouldn't be necessary.

She clung to Toby's hands as he left. "You will write, won't you? And promise you will take care?"

Toby squeezed her hands gently, his brilliant blue eyes crinkling at the corners as he leaned down from the saddle. "You have my word on it, m'dear. No Frenchy is going to get the better of me!"

◆ Chapter 7 ◆

Lucia was restless. Everything in her room served to remind her that by this time tomorrow she would be in London; the shabby corded trunk stood roped beneath the window and smaller boxes lay open, waiting to receive the neatly folded piles of garments.

She turned her back on Chloe's excited chatter and wandered disconsolately along the quiet, softly lit corridors, leaning over to peer down into the cool hall, loving the lingering fragrance of fresh flowers.

At the library door she tapped hesitantly and went in.

Colonel Mannering laid his book aside and stretched out a hand. Lucia perched on his chair and wound an affectionate arm around his neck.

"Packing all done?"

"Nearly"

"Good." There was a strained silence. "I'm going to miss you," he said.

Lucia stood up and drifted about the room. He watched the drooping figure with an echoing sadness in his own heart, but after a moment said bracingly, 'Come now, child, it isn't the end of the world.

113

Would you be good enough to bring me that box you are manhandling!"

The box was made of soft calfskin, beautifully tooled. Lucia put it into his hands, and it seemed an age before looking up at her, his fierce eyes very bright.

"This contains your grandmother's jewels," he said slowly. "They should have gone to your mother by rights . . . now they are yours." He flicked open the box, and Lucia gasped.

"I couldn't possibly . . ." she began, but he wasn't listening. He was lifting out a single square emerald on an ornate gold chain, a beautiful simple jewel which glowed in the candlelight. Lucia glanced up— it was the necklet her grandmother was wearing in the protrait.

The colonel was holding it almost reverently. "I gave this to Marianne the day Freddie was born." He looked up at Lucia, and there were tears in his eyes.

"Oh, Grandfather!" Lucia put her arms around him, and so they sat for a long time, very close, without speaking.

Lady Aurelia Springhope arrived shortly after noon on the following day, and the manner of her arrival was a revelation to Lucia, who first stared unbelievingly from the parlor window and then flew out onto the steps as the cavalcade drew to a halt.

The traveling coach, with Newbury up on the box, was attended by two postilions and two outriders

ers; a smaller coach carrying the lady's servants and most of the baggage brought up the rear.

A young man sprang down, a veritable sprig of fashion, his dark curly hair brushed into a careful semblance of disorder. He turned to assist Lady Springhope, who bounced down the steps like a well-corseted india-rubber ball, her tiny plump form resplendent in purple silk, a number of feathers bobbing riotously over the wide brim of her hat.

Lucia was greeted with brusque affection, and found her breath caught by a vision in pale blue cambric picking her way daintily down from the coach.

Lady Henrietta Elliott was just eighteen—vivacious, headstrong, and quite distractingly lovely, with a pair of merry dark eyes and a profusion of glossy brown ringlets clustered beneath a charming chip bonnet.

She drifted across to Lucia, holding out her hands. "You must be Lucia! I'm Hetty Elliott, Hugo's sister. I hope we shall be friends."

Lucia warmed to her at once; indeed, it would be impossible to resist such open friendliness.

"We have brought Bruno with us." Hetty drew her brother forward. They were incredibly alike. "Bruno is to stay with us in London until it is time for him to go up to Oxford."

"Are we to travel all the way to London like that?" Lucia indicated the cavalcade.

They both giggled. "You know Aunt Aurelia!" Bruno breathed. "A footpad around every corner, a highwayman behind every bush!"

"If you are quite finished chattering," commented that good lady tartly, "I should be glad of an arm up the steps."

Lucia and Bruno assisted the small plump figure to mount to the front door.

Colonel Mannering was waiting in the hall. He had insisted on coming downstairs for the occasion, and stood now leaning heavily on his ebony cane.

The two old friends surveyed each other, frankly appraising. Lady Springhope broke the silence. "Well, Rupert! It's been a long time. You're still a handsome devil, I see!"

The eyebrows twitched appreciatively. "And you, my dear Aurelia, are just as you were—if a trifle plumper!"

She chuckled. "Lordy, my dear man, sometimes I feel a hundred! Ah, Addie! I hope I find you well?"

Aunt Addie, who had been hovering in the background, came forward full of effusive greetings.

She shepherded them, all talking at once, into the parlor. A light luncheon had been prepared, she told them eagerly—just a cold collation that might be served whenever they should be ready.

"Whenever you like, Addie my dear, We are entirely in your hands. I hope we aren't putting you to a vast deal of trouble."

"It is no trouble." There was a quiver in Addie's voice. "After today we shall be . . . very quiet! I'll go and see. . . ." Her voice trailed off and her face crumpled. She scurried from the room, and Lady Springhope raised one expressive eyebrow.

"Oh, poor Aunt Addie!" Lucia rose. "She's upset.

I'll go after her." Lucia returned later alone; Aunt Addie had gone to lie down.

Before the party left for London, the two old friends had a few moments together.

"So, Rupert! We did well, to find Lucia for you?"

Aurelia wondered if he had not heard. When he did answer, his voice was husky. "I do not believe that I can ever repay you. That child has become all the world to me."

"Ah! I knew it! The moment I set eyes on her, my mind flew back over forty years!"

"I want no expense spared!" the colonel insisted. "She is to have the very best—you shall have a draft on my bank. I am depending on you, Aurelia, to do for Lucy what I cannot!"

"Never fear, my dear Rupert! I have a great fondness for the child. You will not be disappointed."

Lady Springhope was as good as her word. Back in town, Lucia found herself caught up in a positive frenzy of buying; she was swamped by material, prodded and pinned and twitched by a succession of dressmakers, until she was bemused and couldn't think it all necessary.

But her ladyship was adamant. Since Hugo was bearing the cost of Hetty's outfitting, she was determined that one should not outshine the other.

Being with Hetty and Bruno gave Lucia a blinding insight into what it must be like to be part of a large family. They squabbled good-naturedly like children, spending every spare minute gambling—everything from lottery tickets to piquet.

Aunt Aurelia's attempts to remonstrate with them

on the grounds that Hugo would not approve brought only gales of laughter, for at home he was ever ready to join in.

People were still drifting back to town, but already there had been a number of callers and the mantelshelf was littered with calling cards and invitations.

Aunt Aurelia beamed with satisfaction. "I believe we shall do very well," she said.

Charles Conrad was among the first of their callers. Lucia watched, amused, as his eye lighted on Hetty; with one glazed look he was instantly and irrevocably enslaved.

They did not see Hugo at all for several weeks. He had taken a party of friends to his hunting box in Derbyshire. When he returned to town he called briefly, and having assured himself that all was well, he considered his duty fulfilled for the present.

Wherever the two girls appeared together they created a stir, so perfectly did they complement one another. Aunt Aurelia would sit on her little gold rout chair, her ample bosom swelling with pride, listening to their praises being sung on all sides and offering up a quick prayer that Hetty would not persuade any susceptible young man to indulge her weakness for gambling.

She experienced a twinge of malicious amusement to see Bella Carew, thin-lipped with resentment! Her own spoilt brat was quite eclipsed—and a good thing too!

Lucia's pleasure was tempered by the thought that sooner or later she must encounter Sir Gideon Benedict, and so it was almost a relief to find him awaiting her one evening as she left the floor with Bruno after an energetic county dance.

He greeted her with the usual odious familiarity, and Bruno, at once assuming him to be an old friend, and having just glimpsed a game of hazard in progress in an adjoining room, said cheerfully, "There, Lucy! You have found a friend and will wish to talk."

He was gone and her path was blocked. "Sir Gideon, be good enough to let me pass!" she demanded.

"Now, now! Is that any way to greet an old friend?"

She was flushed and out of breath from her exertions, and the emerald on her breast flashed as it rose and fell; his eyes fastened on it covetously as his insolent glance swept her.

"My God, you're beautiful!" He put out a hand, and she flinched. It was an involuntary movement, but she knew he had seen; for an instant the smiling mask slipped. Then his teeth were flashing white and his words held an underlying threat.

"I don't see Mandersely here this evening? I wonder, now, d'you think these good people would be interested to learn how you first became acquainted with Lord Mandersely?"

Lucia's heart began to thud. "You cannot know . . . nobody knows! Unless . . ." Her eyes widened suddenly. "Mr. Franklyn! Did he . . . ?"

Sir Gideon was almost purring with satisfaction. "Thank you, my dear, for confirming it! I'll not say how I heard, but . . . a word dropped here and there, in the right quarter . . . it would soon get around. Poisonous little things, words!" He laughed softly. "It could be most entertaining!"

"No one would believe you!"

"You think not? That's all right then." His attention appeared to wander; a speculative gleam came into his eyes. "Is that not Mandersely's sister? Quite devastatingly pretty! A bit of a gambler, too, I'm told. It runs in the family, you know!"

Lucia's mouth was dry. "You will leave Lady Hetty alone."

He smiled.

"What do you want of me?" she whispered.

Sir Gideon smiled. "Well now—a little kindness will do for a start; a few of those favors you've been distributing so freely this evening!"

Lucia's mind was twisting this way and that in a desperate effort to seek some way out. Tell Hugo, Toby had said; but Sir Gideon hadn't actually done anything except utter vague threats, which he could easily deny. If she could just keep him away from Hetty . . .

"We should need to be discreet!" She heard her own voice sounding unbearably coy, his eyes widened. "Lady Springhope does not approve of you. She is already sending me black looks; she would pack me straight back to the country if I made a scandal."

"You have no idea how discreet I can be when I wish, dear Lucia! And I have a way with sour old dowagers!"

He offered his arm with a mocking bow, and

hough every nerve in her body screamed, she took
t. "There is one condition, sir." She gave him an
rch look. "You must promise to leave Hetty Elliott
lone."

"And what would I want with Hetty Elliott when
have you?" Like most vain men, he saw nothing
dd in her apparent change of heart.

"And you will say nothing?"

"You will not give me cause!" he insisted softly.

Sir Gideon led her to Lady Springhope's side. He
tayed but a moment, devoting himself to the for-
nidable task of charming the old lady, a ploy that
net with little success. When he left, she sent a par-
icularly searching look upon her charge. "I need not
ell you, of all people, that *that* connection will not
lo!"

Lucia murmured something incoherent, but the
evening was ruined.

Back home, Hetty collapsed on Lucia's bed and
icked her slippers in the air. "Lordy, what an evening! I'm exhausted, and my dress is ruined!" She sat
up, hugging her knees, her eyes shining. "And so
many compliments, I declare I am quite dizzy!"

She leaned forward. "Who was that divinely
wicked-looking man—the one I saw you talking to
earlier?"

Lucia had been staring out of the darkened windows. Now she twitched the heavy curtains together
with unsteady fingers. "Oh, he was just someone I
knew slightly a while back. You wouldn't care for
him."

To her immense relief, Hetty didn't pursue th
matter; she was much too full of her own conquests.

"Did you hear that absurd boy with the face of a
angel? He vowed he would compose a poem to th
beauty of my eyes! He waxed quite lyrical!" Sh
giggled. "Charles was furious!"

"Don't hurt Charles Conrad, Hetty; I believe he i
very much in love with you, and he's too nice to pla
fast and loose with."

Hetty pouted. "Goodness! What a fuss! I shall b
thinking you in love with him yourself!"

"Don't be idiotish!" Lucia said sharply. "I jus
don't like to see you making him jealous deliber
ately."

"Oh well, he shouldn't be so possessive." Hetty
slid off the bed and trailed her wrap to the door. Sh
swung around with a sudden return of enthusiasm
"Lucy! Let's have a picnic!"

Lucia stared, and laughed. "Oh, Hetty! It's Octo
ber!"

"I don't see why that should stop us. The days are
quite unseasonably warm! We could make up
party: the Bellinghams and Charles, Bruno, you and
me"—her eyes lit up—"and Hugo! In fact, Hugo
can organize it. It's high time he stirred himself o
our behalf!"

"Your brother will never lend himself to such
venture."

Hetty refused to be discouraged. She would tackl
Hugo!

Lucia lay awake wondering what she was going t
do about Sir Gideon. He wouldn't long be conten

ith a few kindnesses; her mind shied away from the
dilemma *that* would present. Sooner or later, Hugo
as bound to find out, and there would be a dread-
l row. She tried to convince herself that it didn't
atter. So that is it? said a still small voice. You are
ncying yourself in love with him! Well, forget it,
or it is the greatest piece of nonsense to imagine
at he could ever view you in that light! On which
epressing thought she turned over and slept.

◆ Chapter 8 ◆

"I'm sorry, Lady Hetty," said Edward Jameson
"Your brother is away. His Grace the Duke of Troo
was taken ill, and his lordship was summoned some
what urgently."

Hetty was furious. She had cajoled Aunt Aureli
into letting them approach Hugo—and all for noth
ing!

"That awful, selfish old man!" she fumed. "Jus
because Hugo has the misfortune to be his heir
Great Uncle Bertram has him running back and
forth at his least whim!"

"Hetty, really!" whispered Lucia in quiet reproof

"It's true! Oh well, we shall have to manage th
picnic for ourselves."

The door opened to admit a very agitated young
footman, who hovered uncertainly on the threshold.

Edward excused himself and went to speak with
him. In a moment he was back. "Would you forgive
me if I leave you for a few minutes? There is a mat
ter requiring my attention. The housekeeper has de
cided to take advantage of Lord Mandersely's ab
sence to have the chimney swept in the gold drawing
room. Being unable to get our usual man, she em

ployed a casual, and now the climbing boy has fallen and knocked himself senseless."

"Oh dear!" cried Lucia in quick sympathy. "I wonder ... may I come with you, Mr. Jameson? I might be able to help."

Edward hesitated. Lord Mandersely would not approve, but Miss Mannering did look sensible, and from the way that her chin tilted just so, he deduced that she was a very determined young lady. On the way upstairs, Lucia was able to admire Hugo's house, which surpassed anything she had yet seen—in particular, the beautiful proportions of the entrance hall, where from a wide cool expanse of Italian marble the balustraded staircase rose in graceful sweeping curves.

The drawing room was swathed in covers. Before an enthralled group of servants, Mrs. Merson, his lordship's housekeeper, was soundly berating a thin stooping man with a wheezy chest.

He was protesting loudly that it wasn't his fault if the stupid little perisher'd fallen down, a'ruining 'is precious lordship's precious carpet—and when he got 'im home, he'd get a proper leathering.

That was all very well, countered the irate housekeeper, but how did he intend to put the matter right?

Edward consulted with Gutteridge, the majordomo, who was endeavoring to bring some kind of order to the proceedings.

The cause of the trouble lay inert and completely ignored; in falling he had disturbed the covers laid everywhere for protection. He had come to rest, a sooty crumpled heap, on the priceless Aubusson carpet. Lucia ran forward and dropped on her knees, her fingers gently probing his head where a trickle of blood oozed.

Hetty, who with Bruno, had followed Lucia upstairs, uttered a shriek of alarm, and implored her friend not to touch the boy.

"Don't be a fool, Hetty! If you are squeamish, you had better go back downstairs."

Hetty protested petulantly that she could see no good reason for Lucia to get involved and muttered darkly about interference.

"Well, someone must interfere!" Lucia stood up, the light of battle in her eye. "You cruel, monstrous wretch! You will never lay a finger on this child again!"

The sweep stirred uneasily. " 'E ain't snuffed it?"

"He still lives—no thanks to you!"

Relief mingled with anger exploded in his old chest. "Now, look 'ere! No slip of a girl ain't telling me what I can and can't do wiv me own—"

"Hold your tongue, man!" snapped Edward. "You will treat Miss Mannering with respect."

"He may treat *me* as he pleases, Mr. Jameson—my only concern is the way he treats this boy."

Her look of contempt swept the room. "Has any one of you even bothered to look at this poor child? He cannot be above five, and this"—she pointed an accusing finger—"this creature has been forcing him up chimneys, which everyone knows is against the law. A constable should be summoned at once!"

This remark drew a fresh tirade from the sweep,

nd pandemonium threatened once more, when a
ool whimsical voice brought immediate silence.

"Dear me! For a moment I thought I had mis-
aken my own house!" On the threshold stood the
narquis, booted and spurred, his riding coat thrown
pack, his face a study of mild incredulity.

Edward Jameson dragged his attention away from
rank admiration of Miss Mannering.

"My lord! We were not expecting you for two
lays!"

"That fact, my dear Edward, is manifestly obvious!"

At a discreet signal from Gutteridge, a footman
tepped forward to relieve Hugo of his greatcoat,
and the remaining servants melted silently away.

The marquis put up his glass. "Doubtless, when it
s convenient, someone will enlighten me as to the
nature of this disturbance."

A simultaneous chorus arose. "No, no, I beg you!"
He put up a hand. "Edward? Briefly, dear boy."

Edward laid the matter before his employer succinctly, and the marquis listened with bowed head.

His gaze traveled to Lucia. "You would have this
villain prosecuted?"

"Yes, my lord. The child is well under the lawful
age and God only knows how many poor innocents
he may have in his clutches."

The sweep called upon heaven to witness as he'd
never knowingly bought any boy under age ... their
parents was rotten, thievin' liars ... it was a known
fact as boys from such homes was puny and 'alf-

starved . . . ?" His voice trailed off under Hugo'
quelling stare.

"I have every sympathy with your motives, Mis
Mannering, but I fear a prosecution wouldn't an
swer." Hugo held up a languid hand. "Believe me, i
would be a tiresome business, and a conviction in
such cases is far from certain."

"Is he then to go free?" the sweep shot her a lool
both vindictive and triumphant.

"Yer a good man, yer honor, a proper and sensibl
gent."

Hugo spoke softly, and the man quailed. "Yo
will leave my house *now*, and I advise you t
set your affairs in order with all speed, for I shal
be informing my very good friend Sir Giles Brough
ton, the presiding magistrate, of this business. He wil
doubtless take such action as he sees fit."

The sweep sidled across the room toward the boy
muttering.

"No!" cried Lucia sharply.

Malevolent eyes snapped at her. "Keep the brat
then! Five pound 'e cost me—and nothing but a trou
ble he's been!" He raised a shaking finger in her di
rection. "If she's yours, m'lord, you'd ought to mak
'er mind 'er manners!" he gasped through a sudder
bout of coughing. "She'd feel the weight of my stray
if she was mine, I can tell you!"

"Well!" breathed Hetty, incensed.

"See the creature off the premises, Edward," sai
Hugo curtly.

Bruno eyed Lucia with awe. "I say, Lucy, you ar
a complete hand!"

Hetty shuddered. "I don't know how you could even bring yourself to speak to that horrid, insolent man!"

Lucia knelt to lay a hand on the child's forehead.

"He has been unconscious for a very long time, my lord."

"It is often so with a blow on the head." Hugo felt the child's pulse briefly. "Tell me, Miss Mannering, what do you suggest we do with this scrap of humanity?"

Lucia was uncomfortably aware of his pensive.

"Well, sir, he needs a bath."

"Of course! Why did I not think of it!" His lordship's lips twitched. "Gutteridge? The boy needs a bath."

Gutteridge digested this information with a wooden expression. "Yes, my lord."

"And a doctor." Hugo added helpfully.

"Oh yes—how kind!"

Gutteridge summoned a footman who gingerly wrapped the small figure in a blanket and took him away.

The majordomo coughed. "My lord? What do you wish done with the . . . er, small person when he is bathed?"

Hugo looked around for inspiration.

"He'll need to be put to bed," offered Hetty, who with Bruno was beginning to find the whole affair slightly hilarious.

"There is a small room at the top of the house, in the servants' wing," Gutteridge said primly.

"Oh no!" cried Lucia. "He would be frightened,

waking up there alone. Surely you have plenty of spare rooms, my lord?"

"Don't be silly, Lucy!" Bruno scoffed. "The lad's like to be even more scared finding himself in one of Hugo's great bedchambers."

"We appear to have reached an impasse," Hugo observed with irony, "There *is* a small bed in my dressing room; why not make use of that, pray? Then if he wakes in the night, I may get up and reassure him."

Lucia turned to him with a brilliant smile. "Why, how very kind, sir! That would answer perfectly!"

Hetty and Bruno fell about laughing, Lucia looked at them, bewildered.

"Oh, Lucy!" Hetty gasped wiping her eyes. "Hugo was funning!"

She looked so crestfallen that Hugo sighed. "The dressing room it is, Gutteridge."

"If you really would not like it, sir . . ."

"I shall survive," he mocked gently. "Though I doubt that my valet will view things in quite the same light. I fear it will require all my ingenuity to prevent his giving notice." His eyes twinkled suddenly. "I have no wish to appear ungallant, Miss Mannering, but I feel bound to point out that our small visitor is not the only one in need of a bath!"

"Lordy yes, Lucy!" Hetty giggled with friendly candor. "You do look a fright!"

"Gutteridge? You will escort Miss Mannering to one of the bedchambers and have Mrs. Merson wait on her there. Meanwhile, my children, we will repair to more comfortable surroundings next door.

Oh, and Miss Mannering ..." She turned in the doorway. "If there are any other little alterations to my household that you would like to effect, please feel free to do so!"

She swept out in rosy confusion.

Hugo ushered his brother and sister into the adjoining salon and sent for a jug of cordial. He took up his usual stance before the fireplace, and for several minutes they conversed on general topics, until Hugo prompted gently, "And your visit here this morning?"

"Lud! I had forgot!" Hetty peeped up at him through her sweeping lashes. "We thought that before Bruno leaves us, it would be a splendid notion to get up a small picnic party."

"A picnic." There was a note of awe in Hugo's voice. "Do you know, Het, I cannot offhand think of anyone else who would contemplate such a venture in October. Still, as long as you don't look to involve me..."

She pouted. "We were hoping you might arrange it."

"We?"

Hetty shifted restlessly. "Oh well, I thought you might. Lucy was sure you would not like the idea above half."

"Was she indeed?" A small smile flickered about his mouth, but before he could say more, Lucia stiff with anger, burst in upon them.

"My lord, could you come with me?"

Hugo stared. "Why, Miss Mannering! What is amiss?"

"If you will come, sir, please!"

Intrigued, he allowed himself to be led along his own corridors to his own dressing room, where she flung the door open dramatically and marched across to the bed. The child lay tucked beneath fine linen sheets; his delicate features still bore traces of grime, and through the mass of golden curls clinging damply to his forehead, a purple lump glowed lividly.

"Lud!" Hetty peered over Lucia's shoulder. "Is this the same boy?" she cried out as Lucia twitched back the bedclothes and pushed up the sleeves of the improvised nightshirt to expose flesh rubbed red-raw; his legs were in the same state from the thighs to below the knees.

"That is not all! Shall I show you his back, where he has been beaten unmercifully by that brute? Oh, I wish I had him here this instant!"

Hugo gazed down at the boy in silence.

"I have been talking to one of your servants." Lucia was almost choking on the angry lump in her throat. "She says he cannot have been a climbing boy very long, for his flesh is still tender; you see, their sores are rubbed every night with strong brine before a hot fire to harden the skin ... and if they will not submit, they are beaten!"

She dashed an impatient hand across her eyes. "Look at his feet! His master lights fires beneath him to make him climb, or prods him with pins." She faced Hugo, tears now rolling down her cheeks. "What I want to know, my lord, is how are such things possible in a civilized society?"

"Civilized? I sometimes wonder if we are!"

"Then why do you not do something about it? you must have some influence?"

He shook his head.

"You could try!"

"Don't try to make a reformer out of me, Miss Mannering!" snapped Hugo. "I'm cast in the wrong mold. As for this scrap . . ." He studied the child closely. "He's no street urchin—observe the delicacy of the features."

"How does such a child fall into the hands of a man like that awful sweep?" Hetty sounded subdued.

"Probably stolen by gypsies—there's a ready market for them in the big towns, and no questions asked."

The head on the pillow stirred, and the eyes flickered open, bright blue and blurred with pain. They moved slowly from one face to the next. His gaze kept returning to Lucia, who was standing in a brilliant patch of sunlight.

At last he addressed himself to Hugo in a hesitant piping treble. "Please, sir . . . am I in heaven?"

Hugo was a little amused. "No, child—why should you think so?"

The boy's eyes moved back to Lucia. "I thought perhaps she was an angel, sir," he ventured shyly.

Bruno and Hetty collapsed into giggles, while Lucia in smiling confusion tried to quiet them.

Hugo, however, gave the matter his serious consideration. "You know, young man, I believe that's just what she is! A truly avenging angel!" A strange expression crossed his face, and meeting it, Lucia's heart beat a little faster.

"Please, sir?" The voice now trembled with uncertainty. "Where am I, then?"

Hugo sat on the edge of the bed and took one fragile little hand in his, smoothing the disfiguring scars and calluses. His gentleness was a revelation to Lucia, until she recalled that of course he was used to dealing with younger brothers and sisters. "There is nothing to fear," he was saying quietly. "I am Lord Mandersely, and you are in my house. You fell and hit your head. Do you remember?"

The boy's brow creased. "Never mind," said Hugo. "Can you perhaps tell me your name?" After a moment, tears of panic welled up in the blue eyes.

Lucia dropped on her knees. "Don't cry, little one! You have had a horrid time! Try to sleep; you are quite safe with Lord Mandersely."

"Will you stay?" he whispered.

"I really ought to go." She looked at Hugo. "Well, perhaps just a few more minutes if you will promise to go to sleep at once." The child obediently closed his eyes, and soon his breathing grew deep and regular.

As they were leaving, Hugo told Lucia she must feel free to visit the boy.

"And now, about this picnic, Hetty. Perhaps you will let me have a list of those you wish to invite. Would Saturday be convenient?"

Bruno stared. "But . . . you said . . ."

"Hugo!" shrieked Hetty, flinging her arms around his neck.

He disengaged himself. "I propose Richmond

Park. What do you think, Miss Mannering?" It was a bland query.

Lucia gave him a long, considering look, and smiled. "I think Richmond Park would be splendid."

◆ Chapter 9 ◆

When Hugo arrived in Portland Place on the morning of the picnic, Lucia scarcely noticed Sophia de Treves beside him, elegant beneath a lace parasol, for the moment the curricle stopped, a diminutive figure was lifted down—a figure in a spanking new suit, determinedly clutching a shiny new ball.

The boy's face lit up as Lucia ran forward, hand outstretched in welcome.

"It's the angel!" he cried amid general laughter.

The marquis introduced him gravely as Master Daniel Maxwell.

"Oh, you have remembered—that is splendid!" Lucia glanced up at Hugo, who shook his head. She gripped the child's hands encouragingly. "I am so pleased his lordship has brought you along. I came to visit you two days since, but you were sleeping. I see you are now much better."

His hand tightened in Lucia's. "Yes, thank you, Miss Mannering."

"My friends are permitted to call me Lucia or Lucy."

"Lucky friends!" murmured the marquis.

She laughed up at him. "You are welcome, my lord—if you are truly my friend."

"It wounds me that you should doubt it, dear child." There was a sardonic light in Hugo's eyes as he swung Daniel into the first barouche and handed Lucia in after him.

The countess had watched this affecting little scene with an ill-concealed petulance which caused Hetty to mutter darkly that she would cast a blight on the day.

That she did not succeed was due solely to the determination of the younger members of the party to enjoy themselves. They endured her sighing and picking at her food and escaped her repressing influence and general air of patronizing superiority as soon as possible, leaving her to retire to the comfort of one of the carriages, while Charles took Hetty and Felicity for a walk.

Hugo obviously found his beloved's behavior less than endearing, for he very quickly came to sit beside Lucia on a rug in the sunshine, watching Daniel enjoying a boisterous game of football with Bruno and Tom Bellingham.

"What will happen to him, my lord? Can he remember nothing beyond his name?"

"Nothing of any consequence, but we shall find his parents, never fear. I am having extensive inquiries made, and with any luck his parents will also have instituted a search."

"You are taking a vast amount of trouble on Daniel's account, sir."

"I am left with little choice, my dear; without a doubt I shall have an avenging angel breathing down my neck if I mistreat him."

"Oh, what humbug!" Lucia blushed rosily. "I believe you have developed quite a fondness for the child."

There was a glimmer of a smile. "Perhaps. He is an engaging creature. Nonetheless, he goes to Mandersely next week. His continuing presence here could prove an embarrassment ..." he allowed a certain dramatic pause "... there are already strong rumors circulating in the clubs that I have had one of my bye-blows foisted upon me!"

"Oh no! How ... dreadful!" Lucia choked and went off into peals of delightful laughter. "I'm sorry my lord, but ... oh dear, how d-dreadful!" She put her hands to her face to stifle her mirth.

Hugo regarded her with complaisance. "I rather thought that might amuse you."

A cool voice shattered the moment of harmony. Sophia stood restlessly twirling her parasol.

"Hugo—is it not time we were leaving?"

"No hurry ... the others are not back from their walk." Hugo unfolded himself easily and with a smile still lingering, he held out his hands to pull Lucia to her feet, steadying her as she stumbled. He picked up her charming straw bonnet, set it on her head, and tied the ribbons expertly beneath her chin.

The casual intimacy of this gesture was not lost on Sophia. Her lips tightened and Hugo, attributing her pettishness to boredom, reminded her in unlover-like tones that he had advised her against coming in the first place.

The rest of the party returned to an atmosphere

charged with undercurrents and it was soon decided that the best of the day had gone and they might as well pack up and go home.

Lucia was beginning to find herself very much in demand as the weeks passed. News of her lovely voice had spread, and when Mr. Brummell himself made a point of gaining an introduction and signified his warmest approval, she was quite overwhelmed by the number of hostesses who requested, nay pleaded with her to honor their own particular little gatherings.

"Individuality is the thing, Miss Mannering," said Mr. Brummell in his droll way. "One should strive always to be out of the common. You have an unusually lovely voice—use it with discrimination, and it will open all doors for you."

Lucia soon became quite accustomed to performing in public, and as her confidence grew, so her voice gained new depths of maturity.

Meanwhile, Hetty was busy making her own mark on society, and in a way that caused her aunt much unease. Not only did she flirt shamelessly with every young buck who dangled after her, but, she had taken up with Kitty Cavanah, a lively redhead whose husband was a noted gambler. Since the pair were received everywhere, Aunt Aurelia found it almost impossible to forbid the connection.

Charles, however, left Hetty in no doubt of his own view in the matter. He told her in no uncertain terms that if she continued along her present course she was courting disaster. This did not please Hetty at all.

"You have no right to coerce me, Charles Conrad!" she stormed. "I am not yet promised to you, nor am I likely to be if you are determined to be so disagreeable!"

"I am sorry, Hetty. I was under the impression that you felt for me the same degree of affection that I feel for you. It seems I was mistaken."

She glowered at him. He looked so stern and forbidding. Her lip trembled, and two large tears slowly welled up in the lovely eyes and rolled down her cheeks.

Charles groaned. "Hetty, darling—don't cry! I can't bear it!"

She flew at him. "Oh, Charles, I am a beast! I don't mean to tease you so. I just can't help being a little shocking."

With this Charles had to be content.

Lucia was having problems of her own. Though still outwardly circumspect, Sir Gideon was becoming more persistent in his demands, and she wasn't sure how much longer she could hold him off.

Every function became a nightmare if he was present, and Lucia was convinced that Hugo must soon hear some rumor. Since the picnic—and with the countess called away to the sickbed of an influential relative—they had been on the most agreeable terms. Much as she desired this happy state to continue, she became so edgy that she finally nerved herself to blurt out the whole wretched business and endure the dressing down that would surely follow.

No sooner had she reached this agonizing decision, however, than Hugo took himself off to see what

140

progress was being made in the search for Daniel's parents. Then Christmas was upon them, and Lucia was able to escape for a while to the safe haven of Willow Park.

Her grandfather eyed her critically and observed that London did not appear to have done her much good after all.

Aunt Addie was shocked by her niece's appearance and at once set about the task of bringing the roses back to her darling's cheeks. It was so good to be home that Lucia bore all the fussing with surprising meekness.

Throughout January there were persistent rumors that all was not well in Spain. The army was said to be in retreat. Everyone waited anxiously for news. At the end of the month Toby came home—an unfamiliar Toby, hollow-eyed and gaunt and disinclined to talk.

At his wit's end, Hugo sent for Lucia. "The lad's almost dropping with exhaustion. I can't get anything out of him! See what you can do . . . he'll never sleep in that state!"

Lucia sat beside Toby, talking to him quietly, gently probing, until, stumbling over the words at first, a terrible catalogue emerged—of a retreat of almost three hundred miles carried out under appalling conditions, of their attempts to embark a whole army under the pressure of heavy fighting at Coruna, and of the death of his beloved commander, Sir John Moore, in the hour of achieving the objective he had set himself.

When Toby fell silent at last, the lines of strain

had eased from around his mouth, and a grateful Hugo was able to bear him off to bed, where he slept the clock around and awoke much more himself. It soon became obvious, however, that he would not be easy until he returned to his regiment.

Lucia was sorry to see him go, but in one sense his departure was a relief, for he was beginning to show an uncomfortable degree of interest in her affairs.

Lady Springhope announced her intention of holding a ball, and very soon had everyone caught up in the preparations. Lucia and Hetty sent out fully three hundred invitations, and for his part, Hugo had engaged to bring along the Prince of Wales.

To Lucia it seemed there was never to be a right moment for unburdening herself to Hugo; the longer she delayed, the worse it became, and to add to her misery, Sophia had returned.

She avoided Sir Gideon whenever possible and resolved that, no matter what, she would tell Hugo the moment the ball was over. She grew pale with the strain of keeping up appearances, and received some very odd looks from Lady Springhope, who hoped she was not sickening with the influenza.

The house became a hive of feverish activity. The large ballroom was scrubbed and polished from floor to ceiling; the crystal chandeliers were lifted down to be washed and burnished to a dazzling brilliance under the eagle eye of Mrs. Barchester, before being fitted with hundreds of candles.

On the morning of the ball Portland Place witnessed an almost constant procession of tradesmen and the air rang with the sounds of hammering as the awning was erected over the front door and the carpet laid out.

Indoors, there were footmen everywhere, carrying bowls of flowers or staggering under the weight of huge potted palms. The two girls, having done all they could to help, escaped into the fresh air.

There were few people about as they turned their horses down Rotten Row. They met Tom and Felicity Bellingham, and the four rode along together, the girls chattering about the coming evening.

Hetty giggled suddenly. "See, Lucy, here comes your mysterious Sir Gideon!"

Lucia looked up with a sinking heart to see Sir Gideon cantering toward them, his great shoulder capes flapping in the wind.

He swept his hat to the whole company and reined in beside Lucia, gradually forcing her to fall a little way behind the others. Migonne shied away from the big nervy horse, and Lucia was obliged to spend some minutes bringing her under control.

"Well, now, fair lady," said Sir Gideon softly. "It seems I am driven to seeking you out."

He turned a calculating and appreciative glance upon her. "You are looking particularly desirable today, dear girl. I confess it makes me . . . impatient!"

Lucia flushed.

His voice grew hard. "I believe you are giving a ball this evening. Is the fact that I did not receive an invitation an oversight, or are you attempting to backslide on our little agreement?"

"It is neither, Sir Gideon," she said quietly. "This is Lady Springhope's ball, and she invites to it only whomsoever she chooses. I fear she could never be prevailed upon to invite you."

It was his turn to flush darkly. "You know, my dear, I grow increasingly weary of pandering to the whims of that tiresome old woman!"

Lucia wished the others had not ridden on so far ahead. "Nevertheless, sir, you did agree to be discreet," she said lightly. "I fear on this occasion you will have to give in with a good grace."

"Perhaps. But you and I are going to have a little talk very soon, dear girl; I am no longer satisfied with things as they stand."

These were the words she had dreaded. He leaned across and covered her hands with one of his own in a gesture of possessiveness. Her heart thudded, but she scarcely heard his next words, for a smart perch phaeton being driven toward them at a spanking pace.

Sophia de Treves bowed graciously as she passed, and Lucia caught the gleam of malicious triumph in her smiling eyes. One thing was certain—she would make the very most of what she had seen.

The feeling of impending doom grew with every passing hour. When Hetty put her head around the door that evening, she found Lucia unusually quiet as Chloe drew her shining hair up into a Grecian knot and coaxed a few tendrils to curl across her brow.

"Are you not ready, Lucy? Heavens! I've got such

144

butterflies ... and you look so calm! Do you not dread meeting the prince?"

Lucia smiled. "He will fall in love with you, my dear. I have never seen you looking lovelier!"

"Oh, do you think so!" Hetty twirled before the mirror, preening herself. She was in white silk, very soft and clinging, with just a simple string of pearls, a gift from Hugo, and more pearls threaded through her gleaming chestnut curls.

Lucia clasped to her ears a pair of drop emeralds, to match the emerald pendant, and stood up, drawing from Hetty a gasp of sheer delight.

Lucia gazed pensively at her reflection, and eyes that were enormous glowing pools of light stared back, deeply shadowed. The emeralds emphasized the clear pallor of her skin, and the dress, of palest gold lutestring, flowed with a Grecian simplicity, its bodice crisscrossed and bound beneath the bosom with silver thread.

She sighed and said that she was ready.

There was to be a small dinner party before the ball, and they arrived downstairs to find Hugo already there. The countess was with him, exquisite as ever, and a model of sweetness; Lucia knew at once that she had done her worst, for throughout dinner Hugo treated her with cold civility, and whenever possible, ignored her completely.

The sheer injustice of being condemned out of and made Lucia furious. Throughout the long reception, as the guests toiled up the staircase, she preserved an air of defiant gaiety, and at the end of it was rescued from the press of young men eager to partner the celebrated Miss Mannering by Lord Alvanley, who claimed the privilege of leading her out for the opening dance.

When Hugo disappeared halfway through the evening and returned with the Prince of Wales, Aunt Aurelia declared her happiness complete.

Both girls were presented and found his royal highness in jovial mood. He had ever an eye for a pretty face, and though in his mid-forties and tending rather a corpulence, he still had a fine presence, though Lucia thought his cerise coat overadorned with decorations and in no way comparable with Hugo's severely cut dark blue.

He was hoping, he said, for the pleasure of hearing Miss Mannering sing—a veritable nightingale, he had been told.

Lucia said shyly that she would consider it an honor, and asked if there was anything special that he would like.

He would leave the choice to her, he insisted cheerfully. Perhaps an aria from one of Mr. Handel's operas ... a ballad or two ... and wasn't there talk of a certain French ditty ... eh? An extremely idiomatic French ditty ... eh?

Lucia blushed and pleaded that she could hardly perform such a one this evening.

"Even if your prince commands it?" he chided her.

Very conscious of Hugo's sardonic eye upon her, she was obliged to yield.

Word went around that Miss Mannering was to sing, and despite her laughing protests, she was all but carried to the platform. She had never been in better voice, indeed several of the more elderly ladies were visibly moved. Finally, amid thunderous applause and with a demure glance in the prince's direction, Lucia announced that she was concluding with a very special royal command. As she played the opening chords, a great roar of pleasure went up.

The prince was still chuckling when she came down from the pianoforte. "Delightful, Miss Mannering! Wholly delightful!" he mopped at his eyes with an enormous lace handkerchief. "You must come and entertain us at Carlton House." He chucked her playfully under the chin. "But where did a sweet little thing like you learn such a song, eh?"

Lucia felt herself growing hot. She dropped a curtsy, murmured something incoherent, and begged to be excused. In her haste to get away, she almost fell over George Brummell, who smiled warmly down at her.

"Well done, Miss Mannering! What did I tell you? All doors, my dear, all doors! You cannot fail!"

It was much later when Hugo came to claim a dance. Lucia was disconcerted, but was given no chance to refuse. His fingers closed tightly around her wrist.

The first steps were performed in silence, until he said in a cold, polite voice, "The prince was still extolling your virtues as he left."

"I am honored, my lord. I had rather thought it was Hetty who took his fancy."

"Hetty is a minx!" said Hugo grimly. "I shall have something to say to her presently."

Lucia cursed her reckless tongue. She had no wish to get Hetty into trouble.

"Oh, come, sir! A little harmless flirting—no more!"

"Something on which you are an expert, no doubt!" There was a wealth of contempt in his words.

They were separated by the dance, and when they came together again, two bright spots of color burned in Lucia's cheeks. "You know, don't you? Your beloved Sophia couldn't wait to run straight to you with her tales!"

"This is not the time, Miss Mannering," he warned softly.

"Oh pray don't let that stop you!" She fixed on him a dazzling smile. "See what a fine actress I am! Everyone will suppose you are paying me compliments."

He spoke through shut teeth. "Well, you have had much practice, have you not? Pray do not strain my credulity by attempting to convince me that what happened was an isolated incident. You have been breaking your given word consistently over a period!"

"Since you have made up your mind, there seems little point in denying it, my lord," she confessed wildly. "I wonder that you should wish to be seen dancing with such a despicable creature! I shall not in the least mind if you wish to leave the floor."

Hugo's grip tightened. "We will complete the set, Miss Mannering. I have no intention of allowing any hint of discord to spoil my aunt's evening. You will act out the part you have set yourself—and remember, the matter was broached at your insistence, not mine!"

Lucia thought the music would never come to an end, but at last Hugo was leading her to a chair, where he settled her and left with a silent, punctilious bow.

Charles joined her and at once noticed her white face and overbrilliant eyes. "Are you all right, Lucia?"

"Perfectly, I thank you, Charles!" Her voice trembled very slightly. "Are you sure you wish to be seen with me?"

He looked puzzled.

"I'm sorry. I am being very silly. Oh please, just keep talking to me while I collect myself! I have had words with Hugo."

"You too!"

Lucia looked up swiftly. "Oh, Charles, you haven't quarreled with Hetty again?"

"She does it quite deliberately, you know. Well, I will stand just so much, but when it comes to flirting with the prince! We all know where that may lead!"

"Charles! Do hush!" Lucia glanced around quickly. "You surely can't blame her for that. Why, he was quite as bad with me!"

"Ah, but you didn't encourage him, my dear—and there lies the difference." He looked wretched.

"Poor Charles! Try to be patient with Hetty. She's very young and high-spirited, and all this is very new to her."

"Those damned Cavanahs are a bad influence!"

"Hetty isn't stupid, Charles. She'll see through them soon enough. Your good opinion means more to her than you think." She smiled suddenly. "What a pair we are! Let's dance before we grow quite maudlin!"

It was turned four in the morning before the press on the staircase eased and the last carriage clattered away. Lady Springhope retired to her bed limp but triumphant, for the evening had received the final accolade of being voted a mad crush.

Two days later, Lucia could not lift her head from the pillow.

◆ Chapter *10* ◆

"Influenza, without a doubt." His examination completed, Dr. Gordon's bushy black brows quivered. "You've been overdoing things, young lady!"

"Nonsense!" protested Lucia weakly. "I'm as strong as a horse!"

"That you may be, but you'll take a week in bed just the same, lassie—and then we'll see."

Lucia felt too ill to argue. It was a relief just to let go and think of nothing but being tutted over by Lady Springhope and cosseted by Chloe.

Hetty was forbidden to enter the sickroom and contented herself by putting her head around the door to commiserate with her friend, for she would miss the great fireworks display at Vauxhall. Lucia managed a wan smile. Fireworks were the last thing she needed; her head was already bursting with them!

The kindness of people she hardly knew was overwhelming. Her room was soon filled with flowers and messages of goodwill, and in pride of place, an extravagant bouquet of pale golden roses which arrived by royal messenger, dedicated simply to "Our Golden Songbird."

Before the week was out, and in spite of protests

151

from Lady Springhope and much head-shaking from
Dr. Gordon, Lucia had removed to a sofa in the
small drawing room. Though still shaky and very
much inclined to dissolve into tears over the least
trifle, she affirmed stubbornly that if she stayed any
longer in her bed she would go into a decline.

She was dozing when the marquis came in unan-
nounced. "Lucia! Why . . . how is this?" He strode
across the room and towered over her. "Should you
be out of bed?"

Lucia stared up at him, her eyes big, dark
smudges in a face of almost startling pallor, her hair
a pale golden cloud about her shoulders. She drew
her wrap tighter.

"If you are come to bully me, my lord, I must
warn you I am liable to howl like a baby."

"Do you think me *so* unfeeling?" he retorted
abruptly, his eyes never leaving her face. "What does
Dr. Gordon say?"

"Oh, he has quite given me up! You could have a
splendid time together deploring my stubbornness!"

Hugo took a step forward and was about to speak
again when Aunt Aurelia bustled in.

"Ah, Hugo . . . Saunders told me you were here.
What do you think of our invalid? Peaky, ain't she?
Needs building up. Lots of good beef broth, that's
the thing!"

Hugo frowned. "A bottle of Burgundy would do
her more good."

"Such presents and flowers she has received! We
are lost for want of places to put them." Aunt Aurelia

152

lia leaned forward. "Most gratifying of all—roses from the Prince!"

One eyebrow lifted. "An honor indeed!"

"If you are minded to discuss me as though I were not here, I shall return to my room," said Lucia in a small voice.

"My apologies." Hugo's smile mocked her gently. He sat down beside her, and his proximity made her breathless. "Perhaps I can make you feel a little better. I would have informed you sooner, but as things were ..." He left the sentence unfinished, and she colored, remembering.

"I did *try* to tell you ..."

"Not now, child!" he interposed quickly. "We will talk when you are quite recovered. What I have to tell you now is that Daniel's parents are found."

"Oh, but that is marvelous news!" she cried, leaning forward eagerly.

"I thought you would be pleased. They came yesterday to collect him. He was desolated to leave without saying good-bye, but I have promised he shall see you at a later date."

"His parents, too, were sorry. They have written you their thanks."

Lucia took the letter, her eyes filling stupidly with tears. "How kind. But there is nothing to thank me for. You have had all the trouble of finding them."

"But you championed Daniel's cause, my child."

"Well, anyway, I . . . am so g-glad . . ."

Hugo took the crumpled handkerchief from her restless fingers and gently wiped away her tears, while his aunt watched with interest.

"Then I hope I may never see you miserable," he chided in rallying tones. "The doctor was right; you are up too soon!"

Lucia quickly recovered physically, though she suffered a curious depression of spirits which Dr. Gordon assured her was a not uncommon aftermath of the influenza and would soon pass. Thus, it only dawned upon her gradually that all was not well with Hetty. She seemed determined to not quite meet Lucia's eye, and chattered incessantly, as though to keep her from prying.

A little gentle probing revealed that she had not quarreled with Charles, and as the days passed Lucia became increasingly concerned, the more so since her aunt seemed unaware of anything amiss.

Finally, when Hetty had picked a silly quarrel over nothing and flounced out, Lucia could stand it no longer. She followed Hetty to her room, and found her sprawled across the bed, plucking miserably at the quilt.

"What's wrong, Hetty?"

"I'm sure I don't know what you mean!" she said in muffled tones.

"Oh, come! You've been looking positively hag-ridden for days. I'm surprised no one else has remarked on it." Lucia's voice softened. "Can you not tell me what is wrong?"

Hetty gave a great sob. "Oh, Lucy! I'm in such terrible trouble!"

Knowing how Hetty's capacity for exaggeration, Lucia sat on the bed and said quietly, "You had much better tell me."

Hetty sat up, pushing back her hair. "It ... all started on the night of the fireworks display ... you missed it, for you were ill. . . . He was so charming ... it was the first time he had noticed me ... and I suppose I was flattered."

Lucia felt suddenly cold. "Who was so charming, Hetty?"

"Why, your Sir Gideon, of course! You must know how fascinating he can be. Before I was aware of it, he had teased me into playing piquet with him."

"Oh, Hetty! Not for money?"

"Yes. Oh, I know!" she said irritably. "I was very silly, but somehow at the time it all seemed terribly romantic! There are so many little clandestine corners at Vauxhall, and nobody saw us."

"And you lost, of course."

"Nothing of the kind! I won quite easily at first; I am very good, you know." She saw Lucia's look of disbelief and said grudgingly, "Oh well, I suppose he was letting me win some of the time, but I thought ... Oh, never mind, the thing is, he made it all seem so very lighthearted, and ... and though I signed some IOU's . . ." She looked quickly at Lucy and hurried on. "He treated it all as a joke and suggested I should play him again to redeem them."

"You didn't agree?"

Hetty nodded miserably. "At the Cavanahs' house. I was so sure I could win!" Her lovely eyes were brimming with tears. "Well, I didn't know what he was like! You never said!"

"And if I had said, would you have believed me?

Still, that matters little now. You lost again, of course."

"He was still quite charming about it. . . ." Hetty was busy pleating her handkerchief. "I don't know what happened—perhaps he got tired of waiting for you to reappear, for he suddenly turned quite nasty, insisted on the debt being settled as soon as possible."

"How much did you lose to him?"

Hetty cleared her throat nervously. "Not much above two thousand pounds."

"Oh, Hetty!"

"It's all very well for you to say 'Oh, Hetty!' " she snapped irritably. "I daresay gambling isn't in your blood."

"Sir Gideon must have known you didn't have that sort of pin money."

"Well, I did tell him and . . . he offered me a sort of sporting challenge. . . ." Lucia waited in stony ·silence as Hetty continued haltingly, "He has a little house out at Knightsbridge. He proposed that I should g-go there and play one last hand of piquet— for the IOU's. . . ." her voice tailed away.

"And if you lost yet again?"

"He . . . he said I could redeem them . . . with a kiss." Her voice sank to a whisper, and she blushed scarlet; even in her own ears it sounded highly improbable. "If you say 'Oh, Hetty' again, I shall scream! Lucy! What am I going to do?"

"Do? You must tell Hugo, of course."

"No!" Hetty was off the bed in a welter of skirts and flying curls. "He would send me home—you

156

know he would. He has already been monstrously disagreeable about my behavior."

She turned despairing eyes on Lucia. "I must trust Sir Gideon; if I don't, he will take the notes to Hugo! He said Hugo would be glad to pay for them . . . and for his silence on other matters. What could he mean?"

"I have no idea," lied Lucia with a sinking heart. "Could you not tell Charles?"

Hetty let out a little shriek, "I couldn't! He would call Sir Gideon out, and I know he'd be killed!"

"So you really *do* love Charles?"

"Well, of course I do! Oh, if I can only get out of this coil, I'll never give Charles cause to doubt me again."

Lucia's mind was working. "When is the assignation for?"

"Tomorrow evening. I am to retire early with a headache, and then slip out. A coach will be waiting on the corner between seven and eight. Effie is to let me out at the back door and be waiting to let me in again. He promised I should be back for eleven."

Hetty couldn't be so naive, so gullible—she couldn't! "Don't go! Hetty, promise me you won't go. I will see Sir Gideon and make him return your notes."

"Can you do that?" whispered Hetty, hardly daring to hope.

"I'm sure I can, for he has employed the shabbiest of tricks." Lucia put as much conviction into her voice as she could muster.

"And you won't tell Hugo?"

"No, but I wish I might have persuaded you to do so."

Hetty, however, remained adamant, and Lucia racked her brains through a sleepless night, but every avenue she explored led her inexorably back to the same conclusion. There was only one thing she could do.

The next day she reassured Hetty that all was in hand, and in the early evening, when they were sitting with Lady Springhope, she excused herself and went to her room.

There, she donned the dark cloak left in readiness, while Chloe sniffed dolefully and protested that her mistress had proper taken leave of her senses!

"Don't be a fool, girl!" snapped Lucia. "Just see if the way is clear and do exactly as I have instructed you."

She picked up her reticule and followed Chloe down the back stairs, narrowly avoiding detection as Saunders came unexpectedly from a room in one of the dimly lit passageways.

It was some time before the truth dawned on Hetty; she left her aunt and ran to Lucia's room, where a distraught Chloe was by now sobbing noisily. Hetty thrust her impatiently to one side, and the empty room told its own tale.

"Oh, good God!" she gasped, turning pale. The maid's cries threatened to escalate, and Hetty slapped her. "Be quiet, stupid creature, and let me think."

But her mind could grasp nothing, save that Lucia had gone in her place.

She made Chloe promise to say nothing, and walked with dragging steps back to the drawing room—straight into Charles.

"Hetty! I thought I would seize this opportunity of seeing you," he said with dry humor. "For when we are out, you are by far too popular!"

She stared at him blindly, and then with a sob she flung herself upon him.

"Why, dearest!" Over her head he met Aunt Aurelia's raised brows. "Come . . . I was only teasing."

Suddenly the whole story came pouring out; Aunt Aurelia reached for her spirits of ammonia, and Charles's expression gradually hardened.

When Hetty finally fell silent, he put her away from him and said sternly, "Lucia has gone to keep this . . . this disgraceful assignation in your stead?"

She nodded speechlessly.

"Where is this house? I must go after her at once!"

"I don't know—I was to be conveyed there and back."

"Ah, wicked, wicked girl!" raged Aunt Aurelia. "I knew your capers would end in disaster, but that you should involve Lucia!" She pressed a handkerchief convulsively to her mouth. "Whatever am I to tell Rupert? How can I face him?"

Hetty, thoroughly frightened, burst into fresh floods of tears, but Charles looked at her with cold anger.

"Don't worry, Lady Springhope," he said in a tight voice. "I shall find her somehow. The house must be known. In the meantime, we must all pray that she comes to no harm."

Hetty let out a low moan and sank helplessly into a chair.

◇ Chapter *11* ◇

The street was deserted. The night was cold and clear and brilliant with stars; a full, frosty moon hung low in the sky, looking absurdly like a yellow paper lantern.

An unexpected fall of snow was already turning crisp underfoot as Lucia hurried to where a coachman was stamping back and forth, alternately blowing on his fingers and beating his arms against his sides in an effort to keep warm.

She pulled her hood well forward as, without a word, he bundled her unceremoniously into the coach and she sat well back in one corner of the musty, shabby vehicle, hardly aware of anything, until, all too soon, it seemed, they were slowing down and turning in at a gateway.

The coachman helped Lucia to descend with a complete lack of curiosity, as though he had done the same thing many times. He jerked a thumb in the direction of the front door and disappeared round the side of the house.

It was quite a small house, little more than a cottage. Lucia stepped nervously across to the porch and pulled the ancient brass bell pull. A tall, thin-nosed man came to answer its clanging, and she was in a narrow hallway. A solitary sconced candle guttered feebly in the draft. At the far end of the hall, light streamed through a partly open door.

"Come along in out of the cold, Lady Hetty, m'dear. I feared you would not come."

It was too late to turn back. Lucia went in and closed the door.

Sir Gideon sprawled in a chair, a half-empty glass in his hand. He made no effort to rise. He was without jacket or waistcoat, and his full-cut shirt was carelessly unbuttoned. From the slight slurring of speech, Lucia guessed he had been drinking—and for a moment her courage almost failed her.

She put back her hood. "It is not Hetty, sir."

"Lucia! By all that's holy!" He tossed off his drink and set the glass down clumsily on the dresser. A circular table stood between them, but it afforded scant protection. "You've come alone?"

"Yes. I persuaded Hetty to let me come in her stead."

"Did you, be damn! How enterprising of you!"

"I have come for Hetty's IOU's," she continued icily. "You played me false, Sir Gideon—you gave me your word that you would leave her alone."

"Oh, come now! One should never be expected to keep one's word in affairs of the heart. You were not there, after all, and she is a taking little thing. But you've no cause to be jealous, me darlin', so let me be having your cloak."

He lurched forward, a muscle jerking spasmodically at the corner of his mouth.

"Don't come near me!" Lucia backed away, keep

ing the table between them. From her reticule she drew a small, pearl-mounted pistol; she leveled it, praying that her hand would remain steady. "Pray do not make the mistake of thinking I cannot shoot, Sir Gideon, for my father taught me from an early age. We traveled a great deal, you see, and in strange houses one is often troubled by rats!"

He flushed at the implied insult. "Damn me, Lucia! Aren't you full of surprises? I declare, you interest me more by the minute."

"The IOU's, Sir Gideon! Put them on the table, if you please."

He laughed, took a package from his jacket hanging on the chair, and pushed it across the table to her.

"There, me darlin', and you are welcome to them. It was becoming a tedious business anyway, but one is obliged to play it out to a finish." His eyes narrowed. "Now this situation is much more . . . piquant . . . don't you think?"

Lucia pushed the package into the pocket of her cloak.

He watched with folded arms, swaying slightly on the balls of his feet. "And what do you do now—shoot me dead?"

"Not if you allow me to leave."

A slow smile twisted the sensual lips. His eyes began to move over her in a way that brought the hot color flooding into her face.

"You aren't going anywhere, little love. D'ye think now that I will let you go, when I have you so exactly where I have always wanted you?"

Panic constricted her throat. She must have been mad to think she could handle him.

"Don't be ridiculous, sir! You cannot f-force me to love you!"

"Can I not?" His eyes burned red. "Well, little ladybird, we shall see ... for I am about to complete your education! We're going to tear away all that damned touch-me-not aloofness and find out what lurks beneath; who knows what delights we may uncover!"

"No!" The cry was torn from her. "You are drunk!"

"Not too drunk to pleasure you, Miss High and Mighty! My God, you've obsessed me for too long! I've a mind to discover if you are worth all the agonies I have suffered! Be sensible, and you might even enjoy the experience." His breath caught in his throat. "Now, put down that silly toy and come here, or by God I'll fetch you."

The gun was shaking uncontrollably. Lucia put up her other hand to steady it, and knew that he had seen.

"Keep away," she pleaded, "or I *will* shoot you!"

With a wild burst of laughter he lunged forward, seized the table, and sent it crashing into the hearth.

Terror gripped Lucia. She strove desperately to remember what she had been taught. With a supreme effort of will she steadied her hand, took careful aim, and squeezed the trigger. The explosion was deafening in the small room; the acrid smell made her choke. Sir Gideon was staring at her; she heard him gasp, an obscenity, and then he swayed and pitched forward, hitting his head on a jutting table leg.

She daren't look, daren't even breathe. The door was flung open behind her. The manservant! Dear God, she had forgotten the manservant!

"My dear Miss Mannering!" drawled a cold voice. "It would seem you have a positive genius for getting yourself embroiled in impossible situations!"

Hugo! Was she delirious? No . . . it was Hugo! How he came there, she neither knew nor cared! Sudden relief threatened to engulf her. There was a loud buzzing in her ears; her teeth were clamped tight to stop them chattering.

The marquis, seeing her sway, pushed her roughly into a chair and removed the smoking pistol from her nerveless fingers. He took out a brandy flask and poured a small amount. Lucia brushed it aside with a shudder of revulsion.

"I'm all right," she muttered through shut teeth.

"Drink it!" he snapped.

There was a strong smell of charring wood. Hugo put up his glass and surveyed the room with distaste; then crossed unhurriedly to the hearth to set the smoldering table to rights. "I infer you succeeded in defending your virtue?" he observed, with a total lack of expression.

"Have . . . have I killed him?" Lucia whispered.

"I doubt you are that good a shot," Hugo said blightingly. He bent over Sir Gideon's sprawling figure. "Hit in the shoulder. He'll live—more's the pity!"

"How did you find me?" Lucia asked in a small voice.

"Lucky for you that I know this house, and that happened to choose this evening to call on my aunt whom I found in a state of near-collapse."

"Oh dear!"

"Quite! If you are now sufficiently recovered would you be so good as to go outside and send Colbert, my groom, in to me."

"What of the servants?"

"They have been dealt with. Pray do as you are bid and don't waste my time with unnesessary questions."

A little color was slowly coming back into her face. "If you are going to be disagreeable, I shall be sorry you came," she said in aggrieved tones. "I have just been through a most wretched experience."

His lordship's voice was cutting. "If you are looking for sympathy, Miss Mannering, you have come to the wrong shop." He held the door open for her, and she stalked through, head in air.

She found Colbert leaning up against the porch quietly picking his teeth and keeping a weather eye on the curricle, where Hugo's team of grays stood patiently enveloped in their own steamy breath. He was a funny, misshapen little man, an odd choice of groom for so elegant a man as Hugo. He peered at her now, open curiosity mingled with concern. "You all right, miss?"

"Thank you, yes." She forced a smile, and he beamed back at her, exposing a large gap in his

ront teeth. "Lord Mandersely wishes you to go in to
ıim."

"Right, miss."

It was bitterly cold, but Lucia couldn't bear to en-
er that awful house again, so she walked about,
rying to keep warm.

In a few moments both men came out, and Col-
ɔert disappeared around the side of the house, to re-
urn almost at once leading a horse.

"It's a bit of an old nag, m'lord."

His tone implied that only as a special favor to 'is
ordship, and because it was in the nature of an
∗mergency, would he be seen on such a one's back.

"I'll be off, then, to fetch the doctor, m'lord." He
ɔouched his hat and rode away slouched over the sad-
ɖle.

"And now, Miss Mannering," said the marquis
ɦarshly, "we will return home, if you please. And I
warn you, do not provoke me, for at this moment I
ɑm fighting an overwhelming urge to lay this riding
ɔrop about your sides!"

"Well, really!" she cried, entirely disregarding his
ɡrim advise. Her breast swelled with righteous in-
ɖignation. "I came here to save *your* sister from the
ɔonsequences of her indiscretion—"

"Which would have been quite unnecessary had
you not been responsible for her association with
Benedict in the first place."

"Oh, how unjust! When I think what I have en-
ɖured in order to keep him from Hetty!"

"With little success, it would seem!" he sneered.

"Well, if this is all the thanks I am to get . . ."

He glared furiously. "For what am I supposed to be thankful? That I did not find you raped ... or worse?"

Lucia glared back. "Don't be so melodramatic! As if I would have come quite unprepared! You are forgetting that I had already dealt with Sir Gideon when you arrived."

"Oh yes! With the result that I am now unable to call the blackguard to book. And pray how were you proposing to make good your escape? Hit the servants over the head and steal the coach perhaps?"

This observation only served to infuriate her the more. "At least I retrieved Hetty's IOU's."

"Which I will take, if you please."

"Thank you, my lord, but I prefer to hand them to Hetty myself."

"Give them to me at once!"

Lucia glowered at him in silent defiance, then slammed the package down in his outstretched hand.

"There! Take them!" she snapped, fighting back tears of rage and almost petrified with the numbing cold that was creeping up her legs. "I know what rankles with you. The truth is, I managed much better than you expected, and you, my lord marquis, are just plain jealous! You can't bear it because I shot Sir Gideon and deprived you of your big moment!"

"Why, you damned little shrew! It's high time that temper of yours was schooled!" He seized her, dragging her forward so ruthlessly that she cried out and almost fell. Hugo swore. "Oh, good God! You idiot girl! You are half-frozen!"

"Of course I am frozen," she sobbed angrily. "What do you expect on such a night? I have not felt my feet for an age!"

"Then if you take ill again, it will be no more than you deserve!" She was lifted high and tossed unceremoniously onto the seat of the curricle. The grays shied nervously, and Hugo calmed them with a word.

He removed Lucia's shoes, commenting with cutting sarcasm upon their total unsuitability, and then proceeded to rub her feet with considerable and, to Lucia's way of thinking, quite unnecessary vigor, until she was obliged to hang on to the side of the curricle and grit her teeth to keep from screaming.

From beneath the seat he produced a blanket, which he wrapped around and around her feet and up to tuck in at her waist. Before setting off, he looked down at her, his face grim.

"I am sorry I am unable to offer you the comfort of a closed carriage, Miss Mannering. I came just as I was, thinking time to be of the essence."

She turned her head away without speaking, and in this manner they traveled home, at what seemed to Lucia almost breakneck speed. She sat very straight, with her head averted, so that Hugo should not see the silent tears that rolled down her cheeks, to be childishly licked away.

When they reached Portland Place, she suffered herself to be lifted down, and marched into the house, head high, very conscious of the lively curiosity of the servants.

In the drawing room Hetty sprang up on seeing

her dear friend, apparently unscathed, and rushed to embrace her.

Lucia put her gently aside. "It's all right, Hetty. I am quite safe, as you can see."

Lady Springhope was blowing noisily into a large handkerchief. "I am very sorry, dear ma'am, to have worried you so. It was never my intention to cause so much trouble."

The old lady sniffed. "Ah well, dear child, thank God—and Hugo—that you are back with us, safe and sound. We will say no more."

"You are very kind," whispered Lucia. "Will you excuse me? I think I should like to retire." Her step faltered as she passed Hugo; for an instant their eyes met, and he could clearly see the traces of tears. With a wan smile for Charles, she left the room.

"I'll come with you, Lucy," cried Hetty. Hugo's voice froze her headlong rush upon the threshold.

"I shall be here at ten o'clock in the morning, Hetty. You will present yourself promptly in the library."

She cast him an agonized glance and ran from the room.

"Don't be too hard on her, Hugo," said Charles quietly. "This really has shaken her badly. I don't believe she will ever behave so irresponsibly again."

"She won't get a chance." Hugo's expression was uncompromising. "She goes back to Mama the moment I can take her."

"Must you be so drastic?"

"I'm sorry, Charles, but I am grown tired of Hetty's capriciousness."

"Look, man!" entreated Charles. "Would you be willing to agree to a formal engagement between Hetty and myself? I am confident she is ready to accept me, and I will undertake to keep her in line."

Hugo stared. "You want to marry her—after this?"

"I love her."

A faint gleam came into Hugo's eye. "Egad, Charles! You're undoubtedly soft in the head, but who am I to try to talk you out of it? I confess it would be a profound relief to get Hetty safely settled ... if you're sure you know what you are taking on!"

"Well, now Hetty is disposed of," said Aunt Aurelia tartly, "perhaps we may learn what happened at Knightsbridge. Have you dealt with that creature Benedict?"

"Unfortunately not, my dear aunt. Lucia was before me."

She stared. "How do you mean?"

"She shot him!" he murmured succinctly.

Lady Springhope fell back, total disbelief written large on her face. "This is no time for jesting, nephew!"

Hugo took the pistol from his pocket and laid it on the table.

Charles shot him a keen glance and strolled across to pick it up. "Well, I'm damned!" he exclaimed with a broad grin. "What a girl!"

"Quite so!" Hugo agreed grimly. "I doubt she will live to a ripe old age. Someone will have strangled her long since—probably me!"

He gave them a brief account of what had happened and of the reluctant admission extorted from the injured and much chagrined Sir Gideon concerning the means by which he had induced Lucia to suffer his attentions.

Aunt Aurelia confessed that she had always been uneasy.

"Then it's a great pity you didn't think to mention the matter to me," observed Hugo acidly.

"Now, don't get on your high ropes, boy! I daresay we all thought it a little strange, but he was always most careful never to put a foot wrong. Ain't that so, Charles?"

Charles nodded ruefully. "I knew, of course, that you and he were not on good terms, but Lucia has always seemed so very sensible and level-headed . . ."

"Ha!" snorted Hugo. "If she is so sensible, why did she not come and tell me the whole?"

"Perhaps, my dear nephew, because she knew that you would jump down her throat if she did!" remarked his aunt sharply.

"Nonsense! Lucia has never been in the least afraid of me!"

Charles decided that a judicious turn of the conversation was necessary.

"Benedict won't make trouble?"

The fire in Hugo's eyes died. "And have it made known that he was shot by a girl! He would be a laughingstock! No, my dear Charles, I think not. In fact, I believe he is about to be urgently summoned to his ancestral home, and I left him with no illusions as to what would happen if he returned."

"Well, I should watch him, nonetheless." "He'll be twice as dangerous from now on!"

It was a very chastened Hetty who presented herself in answer to her brother's summons. She had hardly slept and was sunk in despair. Hugo almost relented at once on seeing her white, pinched face, but he decided that it wouldn't do her any harm to be frightened a little more, so he put on his sternest face and gave her the worst dressing-down she had ever endured.

At the end of it he paused. "I had intended to banish you straight home . . ."

Her head came up slowly.

He held out a hand. "Oh, come here, Het!" She flew into his arms with a great sob, and he smoothed away her tears with his slim white finger. "Charles has asked if I will favor him as a brother-in-law."

"Charles?" Hetty stared, red-eyed. "Oh, but . . . Charles loathes me after . . ."

"Charles loves you, little goose!" Hugo shook her. "Come now—will you have him?"

"Will I?" She reached up on tiptoe to fling her arms around his neck and kiss him. "I'm sorry I've been such a trial! I promise I'll never cause you a moment's unease again!"

Hugo disengaged himself and gave her one of his lazy smiles. "Don't try to be too much of a saint, Het—I don't think we could stand the strain! Now, go along and pretty yourself up before Charles arrives. And, Hetty . . ." He held out the package of IOU's. These are yours. Destroy them if you wish, but I advise you to keep them as a reminder—if ever you are tempted!"

At the door she hesitated. "Hugo? Will you not extend your generosity to Lucy also? What she did, she did for me."

His face at once assumed a shuttered look. "The circumstances, however, are quite different."

"Oh, well . . ." Hetty shrugged and closed the door. Outside, her happiness bubbled up again, and she ran upstairs to spread the wonderful, wonderful news.

Lucia hadn't slept very well either; she had been obliged to endure Chloe's nonstop chatter; the silly girl's relief concerning her mistress's safe deliverance seemed to be mingled with a tendency to regard Hugo as some kind of knight in shining armor—an image Lucia found excessively irritating.

However, when Hetty arrived with her news, Lucia endeavored to put her own feelings to one side and join in her friend's rejoicing.

And in all the general celebrations which followed, no one noticed that she and Hugo were scarcely speaking.

◆ Chapter *12* ◆

At the beginning of May, Toby came home for a brief visit, looking very lean and fit and obviously brimming over with enthusiasm.

"I daresay we shall be off again before long," he told Lucia cheerfully, his brilliant blue eyes crinkling up at the corners.

In fact, it was to be over two months before he left. All through early summer, regiments were marching on Kent until, by mid-July, a huge force was encamped at Deal, awaiting orders to embark for an assault on the Dutch coast.

Parties were got up among many of Lucia's and Hetty's friends to drive into Kent to see the great armada sail. Young Tom Bellingham had enlisted, and the two girls were invited to accompany the family, who were going to see him off. Hetty agreed eagerly, but Lucia had no stomach for such a venture and preferred to go quietly down to Willow Park.

Hetty wrote to her later, full of her splendid adventure. Lucy could have no idea what she had missed! It was just like an enormous pageant, with all the regiments in their different-colored uniforms. "We did not actually see Tom or Toby, for there were such thousands of soldiers, but it was a very gay affair. There were so many carriages and so many people we knew. We had a splendid view as the men were rowed out to the waiting ships; there was martial music playing and the people cheered. ... I wouldn't have missed it for the world!" Lucia smiled as she read the letter to her grandfather, but nonetheless, she was glad she hadn't been there.

By the third week in August the two girls were back in London. Town was empty of people, and it was unbearably hot and oppressive, but Hetty was to marry in late October and there was so much to be done. Charles had bought a dear little house, which was to be decorated and furnished just to her liking, and then there were bridal clothes to be decided upon, in which respect she had to admit that Hugo had been most generous.

The couple were to be married in the little church at Mandersely, and Lucia was to be bridesmaid, in company with Hetty's two younger sisters.

The girls were sitting over an early breakfast one morning discussing the finer details of Hetty's bridal gown when they heard voices in the hall.

The door was flung open, and Hugo strode in, halting abruptly on the threshold. "Forgive me!" he said. "I am interrupting your breakfast."

"Goodness, that doesn't matter. We'd quite finished, hadn't we, Lucy?" Hetty gazed at her brother, intrigued by his unaccustomed air of urgency.

"I must see Aunt Aurelia. The fact is . . ." His eyes rested on Lucia for a moment with an unfathomable expression, then he continued tersely. "I leave for Dover immediately."

Lucia sprang up, the color slowly draining from her face. "Toby? Something has happened. What is it?"

"I don't know." He saw that she didn't believe him. "It's the truth. I have a brief note from a Colonel Prendergast of the Warwickshire militia stationed at Dover informing me that Toby is among a great number of sick men quartered on them. He thought I would wish to remove him as soon as possible."

Saunders came quietly to the door to say that Lady Springhope would see Hugo. Lucia seemed suddenly to come back to life; without a word she rushed past them up the stairs.

Hugo stared after her, frowning. "I was afraid she would take it badly," he said.

Aunt Aurelia sat bold upright in her huge bed, sipping her chocolate as Hugo explained.

"I wondered if I might bring Toby here? My staff are more than capable, but I feel he may be more at ease among familiar faces. You wouldn't need to be troubled. ... I'll arrange whatever may be necessary in the way of nursing."

"Foolish boy! As though I would begrudge any inconvenience! I shall have a room made ready at once."

"Thank you—I have asked Dr. Gordon to stand by."

"When may we expect you?" asked Hetty.

"That rather depends on what I meet at the other end. With any luck, late this evening."

There was a knock and Lucia came in. They all

177

stared, for she had on her bonnet and a light wrap. She was still pale, but quite composed.

"Thank goodness!" she exclaimed on seeing Hugo. "I was afraid you might already have left."

Hetty was puzzled. "Lucy! We are not going out, are we?"

"No, dear." Lucia turned to Hugo, pulling on a pair of soft kid gloves with an air of determination. "I am coming with you, my lord."

"The devil! Indeed you are not! I am traveling with all the speed I can make."

"I am quite used to travel, sir."

"But not with me." There was a curt finality in the words.

"Hugo's right, m'dear," Aunt Aurelia agreed. "It wouldn't do. You shall help me to prepare."

Lucia might never have heard; as Hugo strode to the door, she barred his way. "You cannot refuse to take me."

His gauntlets jerked angrily through his hands. "Miss Mannering, I have no time to waste in argument. Kindly stand aside, and just *be told* for once!"

She stood before the door. He noted the stubborn set of her chin, the appeal in the wide green eyes. "Please, my lord, take me. I won't be any trouble, and you might be glad of help."

Hugo heaved an irritable sigh, looked to his aunt for guidance, and finally said tersely, "Oh, very well, child, come! But on your own head be it. I shall make no concessions to your presence."

He hustled her down the stairs and out to the waiting coach. Colbert tipped his hat to her with a grin, which earned him a sharp rebuke coupled with a curt order to let the horses go.

Hugo settled Lucia and stretched out in the opposite corner, contemplating her grimly. She flushed and looked away out of the window. Only an overwhelming concern for Toby had made her persist, but the prospect of spending so many hours alone in Hugo's company was more than a little daunting.

Since the affair at Knightsbridge, they had scarcely exchanged more than the barest civilities. It was the longest time they had ever gone without some kind of reconciliation, and it became apparent that he no longer had the least desire to affect such a reconciliation. She had finally put herself quite beyond the pale.

There had been the occasion of the Prince of Wales's grand Midsummer Fete, an event of almost exotic splendor. She had received the doubtful honor of being invited to sing, and blushed even now remembering how the prince had pursued her with a distressing persistence and endeavored to press upon her a most extravagant hair ornament, which he had ordered to be made in the guise of a singing bird, intricately worked in gold with tiny emeralds for the eyes. "A golden songbird for his golden songbird," he had said.

Hugo had been obliged to extricate her from her predicament, which had given his royal highness quite the wrong impression! He had nudged Hugo playfully, given him a knowing wink, and hinted that he understood perfectly. The ornament might serve as a wedding present, what!

As might have been expected, this incident in no way served to mend matters.

The coach was now out of town and rattling along at a frightening pace. Lucia sneaked a look at the marquis, but he appeared to be asleep, his body swaying easily with every bump and jolt.

At the first change he didn't stir, except to open his eyes briefly. They rested on Lucia with a disconcerting directness before closing again, and then the coach was springing forward, as the fresh horses renewed the pounding speed.

At the next stage Hugo sat up and stretched.

"Comfortable, Miss Mannering?" he inquired with a slightly malicious smile.

"Perfectly, I thank you, my lord," she replied though in spite of the superior springing and sumptuous upholstery, she was privately convinced that every bone in her body was being shaken loose.

"Would you care to stretch your legs while the horses are changed?"

She lifted her chin. "No, thank you, sir."

Hugo regarded the stiff little figure—and knew that the direst tortures would not drag any complaint from her. His smile deepened a little.

"Miss Mannering, do you think we might call a truce? I really cannot travel all the way to Dover with you glowering at me."

"I never glower!"

"I have no wish to appear argumentative, but you are doing so now," he insisted gently. He stood up and held out a hand to her. "Come, Lucy—it is so hot and stuffy. A little fresh air will do us both good."

His unexpected use of the familiar "Lucy" was her undoing.

When they were back in the coach, Hugo tried to arrange the cushions to afford her a greater degree of protection, "I am sorry if you are feeling bruised, but I did warn you." He pulled a hamper from beneath the seat.

"I don't mind in the least, if only we may get to Toby more quickly. I haven't thanked you for letting me come."

Hugo eyed her quizzically and proffered a wing of chicken. "I wish you will tell me how I might have prevented you."

Lucia bit thoughtfully into the chicken. "I can be very stubborn," she conceded.

His lips twitched. "I had noticed! By the way, I have some property of yours. I was of two minds whether to return it or not." He took the pistol from his pocket and handed it across to her. "It is cleaned, but not loaded, should you feel tempted!"

Her smile flickered. She looked down at the gun and then her clear eyes lifted. "I believe I owe you an apology, sir."

"Again, Lucia?" he mocked gently. "I seem to remember you saying something similar once before."

She flushed. "Yes . . . well, you must bring out the worst in me. I have always been cursed with a lively temper; I suppose it is my Italian blood."

"And did your father never attempt to curb it?"

"He used to laugh at me." Her dimple flashed out. "It worked very well."

"I will strive to remember next time," said Hugo dryly. "But I fear I can hold out little hope."

"I said some dreadful things that night. I was so overwhelmingly glad to see you . . . and then it all went wrong!"

"For which I must bear some part of the blame. However, we must try to avoid a repetition. I should hate to figure in your memoirs solely as the man who first took a whip to you."

She chuckled. There was a companionable silence until Hugo said abruptly, "Lucia, were you really so afraid of me that you could not tell me of Sir Gideon's threats?"

She colored slightly. "At first, you were not there, and I thought I would manage it all without you." Her eyes flicked to his face and away again. "But later it all grew too much for me, and I knew I must tell you. Only, by then, we had established such a degree of harmony . . . I could not bear the thought of incurring your wrath yet again and the longer I left it, the harder it became. . . ." she trailed off in confusion.

"I'm sorry you found me so . . . unapproachable."

"Oh no! I daresay I was just being a coward.".

Much later, when Lucia had been lulled to sleep by the swaying of the coach, Hugo lay back watching her. Her bonnet lay discarded at her side, and now and again a shaft of sunlight through the passing trees would catch at the hair clinging damply to her brow and light up the shining tips of the long golden lashes curving on her cheek.

A feeling of excitement was beginning to grow in

him, as though he were discovering her for the very first time. This warm-hearted, slender girl, who at times infuriated him almost beyond endurance, was his! Oh, why had he not had the wit to realize it from the first?

His thoughts were rudely shattered as the coach lurched to a halt. Looking out, Hugo saw they had arrived. Reluctantly his mind switched back to the business at hand, but resolved that he would speak to Lucia at the first opportunity.

She opened sleep-filled eyes. "Are we there?"

Hugo nodded. He leaned out and spoke to the sentry.

"I don't rightly know where you'll find the colonel, sir." The man shook his head. "There's bloody chaos in there—beggin' the young lady's pardon, sir. I've never seen anything like it! I should try the adjutant's office." The coach moved on.

Lucia looked apprehensive. "What did he mean?"

"I don't know." Hugo climbed down. "Stay here," he said briefly. He finally ran the colonel to earth at the far end of the buildings, but not before he had witnessed scenes of the most appalling misery. Wherever he looked, hundreds of men covered every inch of floor space, helpless, hopeless men shaken with ague, many of them crying like babies in their wretchedness.

Colonel Prendergast wore the air of a man harassed almost beyond endurance. He was a tall, spare man with red hair fast turning gray. Hugo introduced himself.

"Ah, Lord Mandersely! You've come for your

young relative. This is a bad business ... a bad business! To be frank with you, we don't know which way to turn."

"What in God's name is wrong?"

"Nothing short of catastrophe, my lord," came the grim reply. "Reception centers such as this are being improved all along the coast; Moore's old camp at Hythe is turned into a hospital and already has more dead than one cares to contemplate. The poor devils are being landed in their thousands—those who haven't perished on the way across!

"The militia are being hard-pressed to get them all ashore. I tell you, sir, I have never seen my own men so deeply moved as they have been these two days past!"

"And my cousin?" Hugo was almost afraid to ask.

"I fear he is in a poor way. We've done our best for him, but you can see how we are placed!"

"It would appear to be some particularly virulent form of fever," Hugo suggested.

Colonel Prendergast inclined his head wearily. "As I understand the matter, it swept through Walcheren Island and South Beveland until scarcely a man remained at his post and the position became quite untenable." He raised bleak eyes to Hugo. "And so, my lord, for the second time in eight months, the British Army was forced to withdraw."

A very young adjutant put a worried face around the door. "Beg pardon sir, but there's a young girl wandering among the sick men."

The colonel cursed him roundly. "Well, don't

tand there like a fool, man! Get her out—on the ouble!"

The young man looked sheepish. "I did try, sir, ut she refused to leave."

Awful realization dawned on Hugo. "I very much egret, Colonel . . . she may be with me."

The colonel turned a choleric eye on him.

Hugo said wryly, "Miss Mannering is a very determined young lady."

"Mannering?" barked the Colonel. "Related to Colnel Mannering?"

"His granddaughter."

"Ha! It must run in the family! I served under im—a long time ago now. Damned fine officer, but tubborn to the point of pig-headedness!" Colonel *rendergast took Hugo's arm with a sudden grin. Come on, lad, we'd better get that girl out of there efore our Dr. Brent finds her."

They found Lucia on her knees in the midst of inlescribable squalor and the stench of excrement and weating, feverish bodies, gently soothing a poor inoherent wretch, bathing his face with her best lace andkerchief. All around her, hands reached out to lutch at her skirts.

It was only when Hugo rapped out her name a econd time that her concentration broke. He pulled er roughly to her feet, his face livid.

"Lucia! What in hell do you think you are doing?"

"Trying to help," she replied simply. "I was waiting outside, and I heard the crying, but there is so ittle one can do, my lord."

Colonel Prendergast cleared his throat, Hugo recalled himself and performed brief introductions.

"You should not be here, Miss Mannering," the colonel told Lucia sternly. "These men are extremely ill. It is no place for a young lady."

"But I *was* here, and they needed help. There was no one else to give it. It would seem to me, Colonel," she added in stern reproof, "that you are in need of a considerable number of orderlies to set this place to rights."

The adjutant goggled, over Lucia's head the colonel raised expressive eyebrows at Hugo, but only said gravely, "You are no doubt right, my dear young lady, but unfortunately this visitation came upon us quite without warning and caught us ill prepared."

"Lucia, you will come out of here this instant!" commanded Hugo, seeing that she was about to become further involved. "We are here to collect Toby—or had you forgotten?"

"Oh, you have found him! Is he . . . ?" She looked around her suddenly, unable to complete the question.

"I'm afraid so," Colonel Prendergast said gently.

Outside in the fresh air Lucia's control faltered. Hugo, seeing her face change color, acted promptly. "Head down!" he snapped, and held her so until she protested weakly that she was quite recovered.

He looked at her keenly; she was still white, but apologized for being so stupid.

"Are you sure I cannot get you something, ma'am?"

The colonel was red-faced with concern. "A little brandy, perhaps?"

"No, really, I thank you," she said hurriedly. "Please, let us go on."

"You will wait in the coach, my girl!" said Hugo.

"I would prefer . . ."

"Lucia!" There was a threat in the one soft-spoken word.

She flashed him a quick smile. "Very well, I will be good." She turned to Colonel Prendergast. "Thank you for looking after Toby. . . ." She gave him her hand.

He bowed over it with great gallantry. "It has been a delight to meet you, Miss Mannering. I only wish the circumstances had been happier. Perhaps you will remember me to your grandfather."

Lucia looked puzzled.

"I once served under him as a very raw subaltern—I don't suppose he will even remember me."

"Oh, but he will! He never forgets anyone. You must visit him when you have time. He likes to remember the old army days."

She climbed into the coach, and Hugo saw her settled.

Colbert was fidgeting busily with the harness as the marquis passed him. The footsteps halted. Very red around the ears, the groom turned to meet the silent query in the sleepy eyes.

"It's no use you blaming me for allowing the missy to go in there, m'lord," he stated with rough candor. "You knows better than me how she is when she gets the bit between her teeth!"

The marquis raised an eyebrow, half-smiled, and passed on. Colbert took out a large red-spotted handkerchief and mopped around the back of his neck, and his nice-ugly face split in a slow, rueful grin.

The journey home became a nightmare. Lucia was really frightened when Hugo brought Toby and laid him in the coach; his face was ashen, his lovely fair hair dirty and matted. Someone had tried to clean him up, and he was wearing a shirt about three sizes too big. Hugo covered him with the blankets they had brought with them and laid his greatcoat over the top, but every few minutes he was convulsed by terrible bouts of shaking.

Lucia turned despairing eyes on Hugo. "Is he going to die?"

"No, of course not!" said Hugo shortly.

Toby opened his eyes and stared blankly at the roof. Lucia leaned over him. "Toby? Toby . . . it's Lucy."

His eyes focused on her slowly, and he frowned. "Lucy? Shouldn't be here, Lucy . . . ship ain't a fit place . . ." He seemed to have trouble concentrating. "Sorry about this, m'dear . . . not feeling quite the thing, you know . . ."

"Don't talk, Toby dear. Try to sleep. Hugo is with me, we're taking you home."

"Home!" He sighed and shut his eyes. Almost at once they flew open again, stark fear in their depths. "Lucy! Don't let them put me over the side. . . ." He was trying to remember. "They're putting them al over the side ... promise me, Lucy ... they'll listen to you ..." He grabbed at her hand.

"I promise!" she whispered, choking back tears.

Hugo told him that he was talking a great deal of nonsense, assured him that he was no longer on the ship and must rest. Toby managed a weak grin. "Glad you're here, Hugo ... damned silly business, this. ... Oh God, help me!" He began to shudder violently, and they had to hold him lest he roll off the seat. And so the pattern repeated itself for the whole of the journey.

When they at last arrived home, Toby was carried straight upstairs, and Lucia was shut out while Hugo and two of the footmen stripped and washed him and got him between clean soft linen.

Then Dr. Gordon arrived, and she was banished yet again. She paced the corridor outside, and nothing Aunt Aurelia could say would move her. She curled up at last on the sofa near the bedroom door, still in her stained, crumpled dress, and was still there when they finally emerged, the doctor's graying head bent, his face grave.

Hugo frowned. "Lucia? Have you been here all this time? Silly child!"

She ignored the reproof. "How is Toby, doctor?"

"Well, now, lassie, I'll not deny he's a very sick young man, but he's strong, and he has youth on his side." He turned to Hugo. "I believe I have found you a reliable nurse—if someone could be sent to fetch her."

"But I shall nurse Toby," said Lucia in a calm,

practical voice. "I should not dream of letting anyone else look after him."

Dr. Gordon stared. "No, no, my dear young lady—I could not permit it. You don't know what you are suggesting!"

"Yes I do. And I know of your so-called nurses! I will not have Toby nursed by such a one! I am very capable, and not at all squeamish; Lord Mandersely will tell you."

Hugo leaned a shoulder against the wall, watching the battle with interest. "Take my advice, Gordon—give in now. It will save you time and temper!"

"My lord, surely you do not approve this foolishness?"

Lucia anxiously awaited Hugo's reply.

His eyes rested on her quizzically. "Let us say that I have learned to bow to the inevitable. Miss Mannering was certainly not put off by the deplorable conditions at the barracks earlier today. I believe she would have organized the entire sick bay had she been left there much longer! And she was a tower of strength on the journey home!" He was rewarded by a smile that made him catch his breath.

"Hm!" snorted the old man.

"Chloe will help. She's a sensible girl, and there are any number of servants to call upon."

Dr. Gordon capitulated, but insisted she must follow his instructions to the letter and take her proper rest and some fresh air each day—conditions to which she readily agreed and which Hugo made sure she followed.

Nevertheless, for several days it was touch and go

or Toby, and it seemed that Lucia was never absent
rom the sickroom for any length of time day or
ight.

When, therefore, Hugo came quietly into Toby's
oom after midnight on the third evening, to find a
creen pulled around the bed to shield it from the
oft glow of the lamp, and Lucia quite alone, curled
p on the sofa with one hand tucked childishly
eneath her cheek, fast asleep, his first reaction was
ne of anger that she was again taking too much
pon herself.

He stooped to wake her, and obeying a sudden im-
ulse, touched the softly curving lips with his own in
kiss as light as thistledown.

Lucia stirred and opened her eyes. She was con-
used at seeing Hugo so close, unsure whether the
iss had been real or part of her dream.

"This is not taking your proper rest," Hugo
eproved her sternly. "And why are you alone?"

"I hadn't intended to sleep." She swung her feet to
he ground. "I made Chloe go to bed—she was very
ired." She ignored the quizzically raised eyebrow
nd crossed to the bed. "Toby has been so much qui-
ter this evening; do you think that is a good sign?"

Hugo came around the screen and eyed his cousin
ritically. His breathing seemed easier, and the rest-
ess, fractious lines had eased from his face. "He'll
o!" he said abruptly. "Now, you can emulate Chloe
nd go to your bed—get some proper sleep."

"But . . ."

"No buts, my dear. I am going to sit with Toby
or the remainder of the night." He propelled her

firmly toward the door. "And pray remove that troubled frown," he added laconically. "I am well able to manage!"

He was looking down at her in a way that made her feel suddenly and quite ridiculously shy; she murmured an incoherent good night and fled.

By the following morning Toby was fully back in his senses, though woefully weak and emaciated.

Dr. Gordon straightened up from his examination with a grunt of satisfaction. "You're lucky to be alive, young man. Quite frankly, I didn't give much for your chances the night they brought you home."

"I don't remember much," confessed Toby, grinning feebly. "But my thanks to you nonetheless, Dr. Gordon."

"It's not me you need to thank, Captain," he turned with a twinkle, "but is a very determined young lady who is no doubt delighted to have proved this old fool of a doctor wrong!"

Lucia blushed furiously and protested that such had never been her intention. The good doctor chuckled aloud.

"I know, lassie, I know. But I'm not too proud to admit when I've been wrong. If the gallant captain owes his life to anyone, he owes it to you."

Toby held out a shaky hand, and Lucia, smiling a little tremulously, took it and sat on the bed beside him.

The doctor left them, and Hugo walked with him to the door.

"That is a very happy couple we have just left, my lord," he said as they shook hands on the step. "The little lassie must be very much in love with her captain to have nursed him with such devotion."

With this jovial observation the doctor left Hugo and never noticed the peculiar blankness in his eyes, or the way that the skin around his mouth had gone white with the sudden convulsive tightening of his jaw.

◆ Chapter *13* ◆

"You should have come, Lucy, really you should!" Perched upon Lucia's bed, Hetty was holding forth with her usual enthusiasm.

"Lady Sefton was desolated that you were not with us," Hetty bubbled, "and Charles said Mr. Brummell was too! Lottie Travers was the only one who could sing in any way in tune, and we had to endure some dreadfully dull, prosy verses from . . . oh, I can't remember the man's name, but Mr. Brummell was quite cutting about them in his usual droll way!" Hetty rattled on, scarcely pausing for breath.

"Oh, and Hugo was there, of course . . . and what do you think? So was Sophia! Oh, but I wish I had one quarter of her panache! She wore a gown of clinging silver gauze, and, my dear, I swear she hadn't a stitch on underneath! It would have put me to the blush, but she wore it with such an air!"

There was more, but Lucia had stopped listening. She was hurt and bewildered by Hugo's abrupt changes of mood. She had been so sure during Toby's illness that his regard for her was growing; she had not, she asserted passionately, imagined that stolen kiss, the look in his eyes, and yet, as soon as

Toby was out of danger, Hugo went out of his way to avoid her.

Oh, he was always unfailingly kind and gentle with her when they did meet. He was obviously grateful for all she had done. But she didn't want gratitude—she missed the teasing, the razor-edge quality that had been so exhilarating a part of their relationship.

And so, knowing that Hugo was to be at Lady Sefton's, she had feigned a migraine in order to cry off.

". . . I had quite thought their affair to be over since the summer, but it seems he has hardly been out of her pocket these last weeks, and is finally on the point of offering for her!" Hetty's voice took on a note of petulance. "Really, I do think Hugo might have a little more consideration for his family! Fancy saddling us with the abominable countess!"

Lucia felt as though the blood was slowly draining out of her. From a long way off she heard Hetty's voice asking if she was all right and made a determined effort to pull herself together.

With a rush of skirts, Hetty was beside her. "Oh, Lucy! What a blind, clumsy fool I am! *You* are in love with Hugo!" She took Lucia's ice-cold hand and gently chafed it. "Look, I've probably got it all wrong. . . ."

Lucia shook her head. "Not this time. After all, it has always been in the cards, hasn't it?"

Her voice was so full of bitterness that Hetty exploded, "Oh, really—I could kill Hugo! I would so dearly have loved you for a sister. How could he prefer that . . . that , . . ?"

"Why not? She has everything that a man like Hugo would look for in a wife. She has beauty, elegance, she comes of a good family . . ."

"She is a bitch!" stated Hetty flatly.

"Yes, well, there is no point in reviling her—she is Hugo's choice." Lucia had herself well under control now, and there was only the slightest quiver in her voice as she begged Hetty to tell no one.

Several days later Lady Springhope developed a nasty cold, and took to her bed swathed in numerous shawls. She dosed herself with a varied assortment of evil-smelling medicaments guaranteed to alleviate the severest symptoms, which had no noticeable effect other than to shorten her temper; she finally emerged from her room, weak and tetchy, to find Lucia alone, Toby having been carried off by Hugo to inspect a pair of matched grays he was thinking of buying, and Hetty gone with Charles.

After remarking tartly that it was gratifying to find at least one person concerned enough to bear her company, the old lady proceeded to doze beside the drawing-room fire until Saunders came in quietly bearing a letter for Lucia.

Almost at once Lucia sprang to her feet with a cry. Her ladyship, rudely shaken from her slumber, demanded irritably to know what in heaven's name ailed the child.

"It's from Aunt Addie," Lucia said in a shaky voice. "Grandpapa is very ill. I must go at once!"

Lady Springhope at once cast her own misery

aside. Saunders was dispatched to have the horses put to immediately, and to tell Newbury to take one of the young grooms for extra protection.

"I don't like the idea of your going off alone, child!" she moaned as Lucia came hurrying down the stairs pulling on her gloves, followed by Chloe with a hastily filled portmanteau. "If only I felt a little stronger! Could you not wait for Hugo or Charles? If anything should happen . . . a man might be needed. . . ."

This morbid reflection only served to speed Lucia on her way, though, having sampled Hugo's mode of travel, the coach seemed to move with interminable slowness.

As though to thwart her still further, the swaying coach came to an abrupt halt, throwing them both from their seats. There was some indistinct shouting, and two shots rang out in quick succession.

Lucia started up, shouting for Newbury. All was silence, and her eyes met Chloe's terrified ones. Then the door on her side was wrenched open, and a huge greatcoated figure blotted out the light.

"If Newbury is your coachman, I fear he will not be answering."

"You!"

"Yes, Lucia, it is me!" She was pushed sprawling back against the seat as Sir Gideon swung himself into the coach; the thin-faced man from Knightsbridge appeared at the other door. Chloe screamed and went on screaming.

"Shut yer face!" growled the thin man.

Lucia reached for her reticule, where the pistol

lay. Sir Gideon's long arm shot out and dragged her back. In a flash she had twisted free, and this time her fingers just hooked around one of the strings before he was upon her again. With brutal deliberation he seized the front of her gown and rent it in two almost to the waist, and as her fingers instinctively flew to hold the dress together, he gathered up the reticule and flung it across the carriage.

"This time there will be no guns, and no gallant Lord Mandersely to rescue you. Just you and me . . . and some unfinished business!"

Under her horrified gaze he brought a flask from his pocket and removed the stopper. He thrust a hand under her chin. "Come now—drink!"

She tried to drag his hand away, and he laughed. She fought and kicked and struggled until he forced a knee across her body, pinning her against the seat.

"Fer Christ's sake, get a move on in there!" came a hoarse whisper from the road.

The thin man, tired of trying to subdue a hysterical Chloe, brought his fist crashing down across her jaw, and she slumped, unconscious, across the seat.

Lucia's scream was locked in her throat, the hand beneath her chin pushed remorselessly upward. "Nathan gets a bit rough sometimes," breathed the full-lipped mouth, so sickeningly close to her own. "Now, are you going to drink, or must I get him to repeat the dose on you?"

She was forced to swallow a great quantity of the foul-tasting brandy.

"You don't understand!" she gasped. "My grandfather . . ."

"Is probably this minute sitting down to his dinner." She stared uncomprehendingly. "Just a small deception. . . ." he leered.

Strange noises were roaring in her ears . . . his face began to grow larger and undulate slowly . . . and then the gloating eyes detached themselves and swam toward her. Inside her head she was screaming, but no sound came out above the roaring noises; they grew and grew until the carriage swelled up into an enormous echoing cavern . . .

Sir Gideon lifted her senseless body with ease. "Get a move on!" he snapped at Nathan, who was making heavy weather of Cloe's more buxom form.

"She ain't no lightweight, guv!"

"Well, call Percy—only for God's sake, move, man!" Sir Gideon crossed quickly to a closed carriage pulled across the road. He laid Lucia on the seat, closely followed by the two men who dumped Chloe unceremoniously on the floor of the carriage and shut the door.

In the stinking alleyway behind Covent Garden, the sound of a carriage clattering to a halt near the back entrance of one of the better known houses of pleasure to discharge its cargo excited little curiosity. Brothels, after all, were as commonplace a necessity as any other—the gentry had the same appetites as other men. It was as simple as that.

Old Megan, shepherding her own little clutch of girls toward the brighter lights of civilization, paused in the shadows to cast an expert rheumy eye over the fair one as she was being carried across the greasy cobbles. In the sudden pool of light spilling from the open doorway, the old crone glimpsed the beautiful silvery hair shaken loose from its pins, skin like alabaster stretching into a long, elegant neck. She cackled to herself. It was going to cost some swell gent a pretty fortune to pleasure that one!

Sir Gideon followed Sarah Faulkner up the back staircase to the second floor, where she flung open the door to a small room, furnished with shabby opulence and dominated by a huge bed. He tossed Lucia down onto the faded brocade quilt and winced slightly as he put up a hand to rub his shoulder.

The two men carrying Chloe demanded to know what was to be done with her, Sir Gideon looked up and shrugged.

"She's of no interest to me, Sal. You're welcome to make whatever use of her you wish. I've no doubt she's as pure and virtuous as her mistress."

Sarah looked the girl over dispassionately, noting the bruise already beginning to discolor the jaw. Chloe stirred and moaned softly.

"Put her next door for now," she said. "Gideon, I wish you would restrain Nathan's use of brute force. I've had one or two complaints lately from the customers."

She walked to the foot of the bed, a handsome titian-haired woman, tall and curvaceous. She had run this establishment for Sir Gideon for the past five years and had made it one of his most successful ventures. She had a reputation for giving quality, value for money, and had a fine turn for novelties that kept the customers coming.

Her hard china-blue eyes now ran expertly over

Lucia; she lifted the silken hair and let it ripple gently through her fingers. "So this is the little maid you're so set on deflowering!" Her voice was husky, with just a hint of a brogue. "I suppose you *are* still set on it? She'd make a perfect centerpiece for our Festival of Venus later tonight."

Sir Gideon's voice was harsh. "No, Sal. This one is mine!"

Sarah drew in a sharp breath. "I don't know what the child has done, Gideon, but I hope to God you never hate me that much!"

He wasn't listening. With fumbling fingers he dragged Lucia's cloak, tearing the clasp apart, and it seemed that he would dispose of the already gaping dress in similar fashion, when he suddenly stopped and began instead to slap her into consciousness.

Sarah stepped forward and lifted one of the girl's eyelids.

"Get out!" His voice rasped. "I don't need you."

Her shrill laugh trilled out. "You're a fool, Gideon! You'll get nothing out of her for hours! She's drugged to the eyeballs!"

His rage was frightening. He seized Lucia's shoulders, shaking her with terrible force. Sarah's laughter died. She wrenched at his arm.

"Stop it, you madman! God! You'll snap her neck! Stop it, I say! I'll not have murder done in this house!"

Benedict threw her off violently, but after a moment he dropped the lifeless figure back on the bed, drawing in great, shuddering breaths. The red fury in his eyes died to an ice-cold venom. He stood, star-

ing down, muttering half to himself, mouthing ap
palling obscenities.

Sarah Faulkner watched him, sick with apprehen
sion. Only twice had she seen him go completely be
serk. The first time he had killed a man with hi
bare hands—just snapped his neck as though he wer
a chicken! The second time concerned one of he
girls.

She looked across at Lucia and shuddered. It wa
better not to think about the second. God! If thos
stupid women who fawned on him, sighing over hi
ruthless charm, could see him as he really was!

"Sometimes I wonder about you," she whispered.

He turned on her with a snarl. "Don't! I don't pa
you to wonder." He strode toward the door, and Na
than and Percy, who had watched with huge enjoy
ment, beat a hasty retreat. "I'll be back at te
o'clock—that should give you time enough to brin
her to her senses. And keep this door locked. I don'
want any of your customers straying!"

He slammed out. Sarah followed more slowly
With a last, almost pitying glance at the girl on th
bed, she closed the door and turned the key.

◆ Chapter *14* ◆

"She ought not to have gone off alone to face goodness knows what!" Aunt Aurelia had worked herself into a fine state of agitation by the time Hetty and Charles returned, and when, halfway through her recital of woe, Hugo walked in with Toby, she was obliged to begin again.

"With the best will in the world one could not say Addie was at her best in a crisis." she repeated querulously. "If only I had felt more myself . . ."

"Be easy, aunt," said Hugo soothingly. "There is a very simple solution. I will ride after Lucia."

His aunt's brow cleared. "Would you, dear boy? I confess I should be easier in my mind."

Saunders came quietly into the room. He looked uncertainly at Lady Springhope and crossed to Hugo's side. His voice was low and urgent. "Excuse me, my lord—may I speak with you?"

Hugo's brows were arched quizzically as he followed the butler from the room. "Well, Saunders?"

The old man's distress became more marked. "Oh, my lord Hugo! I don't know how to tell you!"

Hugo went suddenly cold. "Out with it, man—don't hedge!"

"The coach, m'lord—it's just come back.

Newbury's in a terrible way ... and young Perkins ..." His voice quivered. "Dead, m'lord, his brains blown out!"

"Miss Mannering?" Hugo forced the question out.

There were tears in Saunders' eyes. "Gone, sir!"

Hugo shut his eyes, and a shudder ran through him. "Where is Newbury? I will see him."

"The porter helped me with him, my lord. We've put him in the little front salon. He's very badly shaken up, poor fellow."

Hetty came flying from the room behind them. "Lord, Hugo, whatever is wrong? You look like death!"

Her brother stared at her for all the world as though he did not see her. "Hetty? Will you get Charles out here—quickly, and if possible without causing any alarm!"

Hetty's eyes opened wide, sensing disaster. "But why?"

"Just do as I ask, please!"

Charles was mystified, but came willingly enough thinking it was some tease of Hetty's until he saw their faces.

Hugo explained as they hurried down the stairs with Hetty running to keep up.

Hugo half-turned. "Go back, Hetty. This is not for you."

She was immediately indignant. "Lucy is my friend! I have a right to know what has happened!"

He didn't argue.

Newbury was perched incongruously on one

ady Springhope's little gilt chairs, his head propped
n his hands. He raised a ghastly face.

"Brandy, Saunders!" snapped Hugo. "Quickly,
man!"

Hugo put an arm gently around the old man's
shoulders and persuaded him to drink it.

When his color was better, Hugo said quietly,
"Now, do you feel able to tell us what happened?
Just take your time."

"We didn't 'ave no chance, my lord. There was
his coach pulled half across the road. I thought it
was a breakdown ... they just rode at us out of the
trees, a big redhaired man and a thin, weasely creature."

Hugo and Charles exchanged glances.

"Fired in cold blood, they did ... thought they'd
done for us. It was this as saved me, though I was
knocked senseless." He fumbling drew out a heavy
silver watch, smashed almost beyond recognition.
"Her ladyship gave it me last Christmas."

"It will be replaced," said Hugo quietly.

"Oh, it's not that, m'lord!" The old man's voice
quavered. "It's them fiends taking the young missy
... and Chloe too! And I had to leave Perkins on the
road, poor lad ... with half 'is head blown off ... I
couldn't lift 'im, you see. . . ." He began to weep
helplessly, and Hugo motioned to Saunders to take
him away.

"Dispatch a man to Grosvenor Square to bring
Colbert to me, Saunders," he added in a low voice as
they left the room.

Charles was trying to comfort Hetty. "This is a

damnable business, Hugo. It was Benedict, of course."

"Without a doubt." Hugo was grim. "Someone is going to have some hard explaining to do."

Charles looked puzzled.

"He has been under constant surveillance since that last affair. As far as I knew, he was still in Ireland. He must have given my men the slip." He frowned. "I suppose I must go up and tell Aunt Aurelia . . . and Toby. I don't quite know how I am going to break the news to Toby."

They both stared at him, Hetty's tears momentarily checked.

"But why?" she gasped. "Oh, he'll be dreadfully upset, of course, we all are, but . . ."

"You must have seen the way things are between them?"

"Oh, Hugo, what nonsense! Why, Lucia has been eating her heart out for you these weeks past!"

A slight flush marked Hugo's cheek. "No! You are mistaken."

Hetty stamped her foot, "I am not mistaken! I tell you, Lucia was heartbroken when she learned you were to offer for Sophia."

Hugo seized her arm, his eyes blazing. "When she heard *what*?"

"Let go, Hugo! You're hurting! We . . . I was told quite definitely . . ."

"Then you were misinformed!" He released Hetty abruptly and passed a hand across his eyes. "Oh! What a damn fool I've been!"

"I promised her I wouldn't say anything," Hetty

ailed, "but it don't signify now." Her sobs began fresh.

Charles took her in his arms, but Hugo snapped at there was no time to indulge in histrionics. Aunt Aurelia is going to need all your support. ull yourself together, for God's sake, while Charles nd I take a look at the coach."

Here, the signs of a struggle were all too evident. green strapped sandal lay tumbled upon the floor, nd in one corner, wedged halfway behind a cush-on, they came upon Lucia's reticule. Hugo retrieved and took out the little pearl-mounted pistol. They ooked at it, and at each other.

Charles wrinkled his nose. "Brandy?"

"Drugged, most likely."

"Oh God!"

A gleam of hope came into Hugo's eyes. "Don't be oo distressed, my dear Charles; it could be the sav-ig of her, if we can just find her quickly!"

Colbert rode in at the gate, and Hugo spent everal minutes explaining what he required of him, nen Colbert was away, grim-faced.

Aunt Aurelia took the news badly. She fell back gainst her cushions, and Hetty rushed across to pick p her vinaigrette and hold it under her nose.

Toby dashed his hat to the ground. "The unspeak-ble swine! You'll have him this time, Hugo?"

Hugo, watching him, was reassured; Toby was hite and shaken, but it was the reaction of a very ear friend, not of a lover.

"He won't escape. But we must find Lucia first."

Aunt Aurelia moaned. "Oh, what must that poor

child be suffering?" She sat bolt upright. "And what of Rupert? Was it all a hoax?"

Hugo's eyes lighted on Lucia's discarded letter. He snatched it up and held it out to his aunt. "Is that Addie Mannering's hand?"

She shook her head, looking suddenly old and frightened.

"Then I think we may assume that the colonel is in his usual health."

Toby and Charles had fallen to discussing where Sir Gideon might have taken Lucia. The house at Knightsbridge and his rooms in Chelsea were discarded as being too obvious.

"Bruton Street—Franklyn's place?" Toby suggested hopefully.

"I think not." Hugo glanced significantly at his aunt. "I think we had best go downstairs—work the thing out properly." He bent to kiss her tear-ravaged cheek. "Try not to worry, my dear. We shall get Lucia back safe and sound."

Downstairs, he said in a low voice, "I have a great fear of where Benedict might have taken her!"

The two men stared at him in dawning horror.

"He wouldn't!" breathed Charles.

"Well, think, man!" said Hugo savagely. "Put yourself in his place! Where better to hide a girl you don't want found? The devil of it is, where do we begin? With a good half-dozen high-class brothels to his credit, and God knows how many cesspools of vice besides, Lucia could be anywhere!"

"Then we don't have a chance." There was despair in Toby's voice.

"On the contrary, we have a very good chance. I'm pinning my hope on Colbert. He has a way of nosing out information. Meanwhile . . ." Hugo eyed the other two grimly. "I want Benedict found—discreetly. If, Lucia has been drugged, he will be obliged to cool his heels for a while."

Toby choked, but Hugo continued evenly. "We'll split up. If ... When he is found, I want him followed and his every move reported."

"And if he is not to be found?" Charles voiced the unspoken fear.

"Then we think again." Hugo's voice was harsh. "Toby, are you not tired out, dear boy? I am forgetting you are still convalescent."

Toby swore and declared he was more likely to suffer a relapse if he was forced to remain inactive. And so they dispersed. In less than an hour Toby was back, chafing with impatience until Hugo appeared.

"I've found the swine! In the Nonesuch, with ... guess who? Friend Franklyn!"

"Did they see you?"

Toby stretched out in a chair. "Oh yes, by jove! Damn me, if you'd seen the smirk on his face! Took me all my time not to smash it down his throat! Don't worry"—he put up a hand as Hugo's brows came together—"I didn't move so much as a whisker! They left together shortly afterwards, walking toward Bruton Street. My men are on to them."

Toby sat up suddenly. "D'ye think we've been barking up the wrong tree, that Lucia is at Bruton Street after all?"

Hugo drew out his snuffbox, "I don't know. Every instinct tells me not, and yet . . ."

Charles came in, and they explained the situation.

"Can we afford to ignore the possibility?" he queried.

"You are right, of course," said Hugo briskly. "We go to Bruton Street. If Lucia isn't there, we'll choke the truth out of Benedict. I'll leave word for Colbert."

On the front step they were almost sent flying by Colbert, who had ridden like a man possessed from a small seedy hostelry in Cheapside.

"I've found her, m'lord!" he gasped. "Leastways, I know where she is!"

Hugo dragged him into the hall, his eyes ablaze "You are sure, man?"

"Sure certain, m'lord! You see, I know this place where that Benedict's fat pig of a coachman likes to take 'is tipple, so I goes there, and in he comes. Well he don't remember me, see." The ugly face split into a toothy grin. "So I plies 'im with a few drinks and lets slip a few pertinent questions, and in no time he's spillin' the lot!"

Colbert was enjoying himself.

"Get on with it, man!" roared Toby.

"Yes, sir. Well, it was a great joke, d'ye see. Seemingly old Benedict give our missy a whopping over dose of laudanum or some such, and she was spark out, so 'e couldn't have 'is way with her. . . ."

Colbert caught the expression on the marquis'

210

ce and blanched. "Sorry, me lord. No offense intend-
d."

"Go on," said Hugo evenly.

"Yes, sir. Well, I kidded him along and got 'im to
ough where it was they'd taken the missy—the Cor-
ir, in Great Russell Street—and 'e ain't there, 'cos
ercy saw him leave."

Hugo let his breath go in a deep sigh. "Thank
ou, Colbert."

"That's all right, me lord. Are ye going to get her
ut of there then, me lord?"

"Yes, Colbert, we are. We'll take my aunt's town
ach. Have the horses put in. Oh, and Colbert . . . ?"

"Yes, me lord?" The little man waited, his wide
oulders and long arms making him look for all the
orld like an inquisitive monkey.

"There is no chance of this character rumbling
ou and warning his employer?"

"Funny as you should arsk, sir! Same thought had
ossed my mind, only as things turned out, he had a
ery nasty accident on his way 'ome. Dead drunk, 'e
as—fell into a rain butt, head-first! I tried to get
m out, of course, me lord, but he was a big man."

"Most unfortunate!"

"Yes, me lord." Colbert met the gleam in Hugo's
ye with a look of pious innocence and hurried
way.

"That's quite a man you have!" breathed Charles
 awe.

"Oh, Colbert's an original—I wouldn't change him
r all your smart-liveried johnnies!"

Hugo looked at the other two, and the light of hope, carefully suppressed, was in his eyes. Colber brought the coach smartly up to the gates. "Well, my friends, shall we go?"

◆ Chapter 15 ◆

Lucia fought against the pull of returning con-
ciousness, as though sensing that with it would
ome some awful, nameless horror. Her eyes flickered
pen at last to half-darkness and unfamiliar walls; a
ingle candle on the mantelshelf sent dark shapes
eaping in a mirror at the foot of the bed.

In her nostrils there was an overpowering smell of
heap perfume, and waves of nausea threatened to
ngulf her. Trembling, drenched in perspiration,
he tried to call for Chloe, but her voice was a pa-
hetic croak in the silence.

And then she remembered. Panic suffocated her,
nd she sat up. A thousand jagged needles seemed to
xplode in her head. Nausea welled up again into
er dry, aching throat, and she sank back.

She lay quite still, trying to pull herself together.
Once again, she set her teeth and raised herself,
waited for the giddiness to subside, and swung her feet
o the floor. She stood up, swaying; where her legs
hould have been, there was a woolly sensation, and
he found herself crumbling into an ignominious
eap.

Sobbing with frustration, sick and dizzy, she
dragged herself to the door. It was locked!

In despair she turned to the window. The panes were small and incredibly dirty. Somewhere below a dog was howling. A door opened, spilling out a sudden shaft of light onto a huddle of crumbling buildings; a bowl of slops was thrown, and the dog's howl turned to an indignant yelping. There was a shout of laughter, and the door closed, leaving Lucia with an overwhelming feeling of isolation.

She sank back on her heels, and leaned her head against the window-edge. Dear God! If she didn't feel so ill!

She tensed suddenly, clutching at the gaping front of her dress. The key was turning in the lock!

A woman stood in the doorway, holding high a glowing lamp—an extraordinary vision dressed in some exotic eastern costume, her hair burnished like copper in the soft lamplight.

"Oh, so you've come around at last!" It was like some hideous nightmare. The woman placed the lamp on a small table and shut the door. "Feeling a bit groggy, are you, dearie?"

Lucia's throat ached abominably. "Chloe?"

"The maidservant? She's safe enough."

"Where am I?"

Sarah Faulkner's laugh trilled out. "Well, now, dear, if I was to tell you, I doubt you'd understand."

It was a few seconds before the full impact of this innuendo penetrated Lucia's weary brain; her eyes slowly widened with horror. She hauled herself to her feet and stood clinging to the curtain, willing her legs not to buckle.

"Oh! So you're not as green as I thought!" Sarah

epped forward. "I think you'd best lie down
gain."

Lucia thrust her away.

"Please! You must help me! I have to get away.
Hugo will never find me here ... no one will ever
nd me here!"

Sarah chuckled dryly. "I rather think that was the
dea! Come along, now, be sensible. Gideon would
ave my life if you weren't here when he returned!"

Lucia shuddered at the mention of Sir Gideon,
nd Sarah half-lead, half-carried the protesting girl
ack to the bed, finding herself unexpectedly moved
y the almost birdlike fragility of the slight figure.

She turned away, closing her mind to the thought
f what Gideon could do to such a delicate, gentle
reature.

"I'll get you some strong coffee," she said abruptly.

"You won't help me?"

It was a hopeless statement of fact. Sarah cursed.
n all her years in the business she'd never felt this
wful sense of betrayal. It was a hard, cruel world; it
asn't her fault that this silly child had got involved.
f only she wouldn't lie there so still, her jaw clamped
ight and those big eyes like dark, tragic pools, re-
roaching her!

Sarah sat down abruptly. Under the heavy Orien-
al makeup her face was haggard.

"Sorry, dear, I'd like to help you, but I daren't! I
asn't exaggerating—Gideon really would kill me!
've never seen him obsessed as he is by you." She
ook Lucia's ice-cold hand and there was sudden ur-
ency in her words. "Will you take a bit of advice

from an old pro, dearie? Don't make him angry!"
She hesitated. "He'll ... likely give you a bit of a
rough time, but for God's sake don't provoke him!"

Sarah stood up, unable any longer to look into the
stiff white face. "I'll get that coffee," she muttered.

As she neared the second floor, sounds of
restiveness assailed her ears. In the large salon her
invited guests, many of them important and influential people, were growing restless. If she didn't get
the festival started soon, there would be trouble. She
suddenly felt sick to the stomach of catering to the
salacious appetites of her clients—lecherous, whoring
beasts, the lot of them—and the women who came
were something worse! Oh, damn Gideon for
bringing that girl! And damn the girl for making
Sarah Faulkner feel as she hadn't felt in a very long
time!

In the foyer more angry voices were being raised.
A pox on trouble; why did it all have to come at
once! She found Sam Preevy, her burly doorman,
and Connell Quinn, her cousin, engaged in a heated
altercation with three gentlemen, one of whom she
vaguely recognized.

Connell came hurrying across. "Trouble, Sal!" he
warned. "The tall, saturnine one is Mandersely. He's
in hot pursuit of that chit Gideon saddled us with. I
knew no good would come of it!"

Mandersely! But of course! Sarah knew enough of
him to feel a sudden unease; she put on her
brightest smile and crossed the hall to confront him.

"Lord Mandersely. I am Sarah Faulkner; how may
I help you?"

He turned, his glass taking in the full garishness of her costume. His lip curled very slightly, and Sarah stiffened, her hands clenched at her side.

"You have a young lady and her maid held here under duress," he said at last. "I am come to relieve you of them."

"Oh, come, my lord!" she trilled archly. "You gentlemen are all the same! The times I have heard such a tale!" She ignored Connell's frantic signals. "We have many young ladies here—most of them ready and willing to please in any number of ways. Of course, one or two are ... reluctant at first; some gentlemen prefer it that way. So if there is a special kind of girl you require, I am sure we can accommodate you!"

Toby swore a mighty oath, but the marquis just looked at Sarah for a full half-minute without speaking—ample time for her to reflect nervously that she had never seen such cold eyes in any man she had ever met.

Finally he said softly, "Shall we begin again, madam? I must warn you that I am not a patient man; since I would not dream of insulting your intelligence, pray do not insult mine! You know the girl of whom I speak."

She avoided meeting those eyes. "You are mistaken, my lord—I cannot help you."

The marquis sighed. "Mrs. Faulkner, you disappoint me! Now, understand this!" Every word fell like chipped ice. "If I must, I will break every bone in your lovely body, and I will tear this house apart, brick by bawdy brick, until I find her!"

217

Quinn and Sam Preevy moved forward to find themselves looking down the barrels of a pistol.

Sarah knew that further evasion was useless. She waved her henchmen away and led the way upstairs.

On the second floor the noise increased in volume, and erupted suddenly as a door opened and an elderly gentleman tottered out, his cravat violently askew.

He hailed Sarah petulantly. "I say, Sal! When does this precious entertainment begin? Your guests grow damned weary of waiting." He spied Hugo. "Stop me, Mandersely! Didn't think this was in your line of country!"

He sidled up. "Heard about this festival, eh, m'boy? Egad, you're in for a rare treat!" He leered wickedly. "Pagan fertility rights—the lot! These Polynesian natives, or whatever, have some damned rum practices, if Sal ain't havin' us on! Quite unbelievable, eh, Sal?"

Hugo's mouth was set in a rigid line. With heightened color Sarah bundled the old duke back into the salon, saying that she would come directly.

On the third floor she turned the key in the lock and said abruptly, "I am glad you came, my lord. She has not been harmed."

He stood into the room and checked momentarily at the sight of Lucia lying on the huge bed, seemingly unconscious, her face was pale as death, her dress distressingly awry. His eyes blazed as he moved forward.

Lucia lay motionless, her eyes tight shut. She had been waiting for a very long time, or so it seemed.

Once or twice the door handle had been rattled, and each time she had tensed, choking on her fear.

Now the time had come, for she knew it was not the woman who had entered. With a great feeling of calm she acknowledged that life, as she had known it for the last few months, was at an end. She could never face her grandfather, or the dear friends she had made, after this! Of Hugo, she could not bear to think at all.

She had resolved to endure what must be endured, without the indignity of a struggle, and afterwards she would kill herself!

And yet, the moment the hands closed on her, every instinct revolted and she was fighting like a wildcat! Someone was shouting her name, but she was beyond listening. She was being shaken, and suddenly, unbelievably, it was Hugo's voice shouting, "Lucy! For God's sake open your eyes. Lucy! Do you hear me?"

He really was there! She clung to him, incoherent and torn apart by wild, uncontrollable sobs. He wrapped her cloak around her and lifted her high in his arms. Grim-faced and silent, Toby and Charles stood aside to let him pass. He faced Sarah Faulkner, and his voice grated. "The maidservant?"

The door of the next room was flung back, and Hugo called Chloe's name; slowly a pathetic and incongruous figure in a bizarre harem costume crept forward.

"Oh, my lord! Oh, sir!" she wailed, trying to cover herself with her hands. No amount of powder and paint could disguise the bruised and swollen jaw.

Hugo's face was like granite. "Madam. This child has a cloak."

Casting him a glance of pure hatred, Sarah disappeared into the room and returned with the cloak, which Charles wrapped around Chloe, keeping a comforting arm around her shaking shoulders as they were led in silence down the back stairs.

And then they were out in the fresh air, and Sarah Faulkner was left to pull together the shattered remains of a disastrous evening and somehow face Sir Gideon.

Colbert drove back to Portland Place at a bruising pace. The only sounds inside the coach were Lucia's racking sobs, which showed no sign of abating.

To see his dear, proud girl so reduced appalled Hugo; he held her close, soothing her with quiet words, but in his heart, there was black murder.

"Wait!" He rapped the order at Colbert and carried Lucia into the house and up the stairs.

The door of the small drawing room flew open, and Hetty cried, "Aunt Aurelia! It's Hugo, and he's got Lucia!"

There was a faint cry from inside the room as Hetty ran to the head of the stairs. With questions ringing in his ears, Hugo walked rapidly on to Lucia's room and laid her down on the bed, gently loosening the hands still clutching at his coat.

"You're home now," he said in a quiet, clear voice. "Hetty is here to look after you." He turned to his sister. "I believe her to be no more than badly frightened, but get Dr. Gordon. He'll need to take a look at Chloe, too."

The look on his face scared Hetty. She grabbed at his sleeve, but he brushed her aside.

In the doorway of the drawing room Lady Spring-hope stood clinging to Charles, a handkerchief pressed to her lips. Hugo seemed to collect himself, stopped, and took her hands. "She's quite safe now," he said gently. "He'll never get another chance to hurt her."

Aunt Aurelia nodded, unable to speak.

Striding across the hall toward the front door, Hugo became aware of Toby keeping step beside him. There were unmistakable signs of strain in his young cousin's face. He stopped and laid a hand lightly on his shoulder.

"Go and rest now, dear boy. You have played your part magnificently, but I can see that you are quite worn out. I would not have your relapse upon my conscience. What remains to be done, only I can do."

"I shall hold up a little longer," said Toby with quiet determination. "You are not going to that house alone!"

Hugo frowned, and then, with the faintest of smiles, they turned together and walked on.

Colbert was instructed to stop at Grosvenor Square, where Hugo vanished inside the house, to reappear in a very short space of time with a pair of dueling rapiers tucked firmly under his arm.

Edward Jameson hurried out onto the step in his wake.

"My lord?"

Hugo swung around, impatience darkening his face.

"Miss Mannering, my lord?"

"She is safe."

"Thank God!" The young secretary eyed the rapiers with foreboding. "Sir, if you will forgive me for saying so, I am sure that is not altogether wise."

Hugo said with icy hauteur, "I do not believe I expressed any desire to listen to your opinions."

"No, my lord." Edward flushed. "My concern for you is solely lest, in your present, wholly understandable frame of mind, you might be constrained to act recklessly."

The eyebrows rose incredulously. "You're full of words, aren't you, lad?" The boyish grin flashed out for a moment. "But you should know, I am never reckless!"

"No, sir?" Edward permitted himself a small answering smile, but insisted urgently, "Do be careful!"

"My dear Edward, I have every intention of so being!" drawled the marquis with a return of his old urbanity. He turned and ran lightly down the steps to the waiting coach.

Toby also eyed the rapiers with a jaundiced eye. "Damned if I can see why you need to take a chance like that. Shoot him like the mad dog he is, I say!"

"How very crude!" murmured his lordship.

"Aye, maybe, but it's also very final!"

"My way will be just as final, I promise you!" Hugo's voice had dropped so low that Toby could scarcely hear, yet he found himself giving an involuntary shiver.

In Bruton Street the two men Toby had left on watch detached themselves from the railings and

traightened up respectfully. There had been no
comings or goings, they reported. The house had
been quiet as the grave. Hugo smiled grimly.

The lackey who opened the door was disconcerted
to find himself hustled backwards into the hall.

"Your master!" ordered Hugo. "Get him out
here—alone. And take particular care not to alarm
his guest, if you know what is good for you!"

The servant had no intention of playing the hero.
Franklyn commanded very little loyalty or respect
below stairs.

Mr. Franklyn came almost at once from a room at
the rear of the hall, lurching slightly and grumbling
at being disturbed. He peered forward, and seeing
them half-turned back, alarm flickering in his bloodshot eyes.

"Don't!" snapped Toby. His pistol was aimed un-
waveringly at Franklyn's bulging stomach. "You and
I are going to bear one another company while my
cousin here completes a little unfinished business."

Toby hooked a chair forward with his foot and
stretched out in it; Franklyn crouched like a quivering jelly against the stairwell; of the servant, there
was no sign. Toby grinned whimsically at Hugo, and
besought him to take care.

Hugo walked quickly to the room, and the door
closed quietly behind him.

Sir Gideon sprawled inelegantly at the far end of
a dining table strewn with the untidy remains of a
meal. His coat was open, his cravat tugged loose. He
was engaged in the dissection of a peach, peeling it

with a slow, sensual relish; he didn't bother to look up.

"Did you ever think, now, Jasper, how a ripe peach is like a beautiful woman!" A chuckle echoed deep in his throat as the full lips closed around a particularly lush segment. "And this is not the only sweet fruit I shall be tasting this night, eh, my friend?"

When there was no reply, he glanced up, and his hand froze in midair. The marquis of Mandersely was standing with his back against the door, looking like the wrath of God! Benedict half-rose in his chair, a bolt of fear running through him; then he sank back, his glance narrowing.

"Well, now, I suppose your young cousin ran straight to you with the news of my return." The full lips curled sardonically. "I slipped your guards pretty well, think you not?"

Hugo made no reply. He turned the key in the lock without hurry and dropped it into his pocket. In a single gesture he swept the dishes from one end of the table, laying the two rapiers neatly in the cleared space.

Slowly and deliberately he began to remove his coat.

Sir Gideon watched with growing unease. "What the devil are you at, Mandersely? Have you taken leave of your senses? Forcing your way into Jasper's house in this extraordinary manner? Where *is* Jasper?"

Hugo sat down. He took off his top boots and set them neatly to one side. "Your friend is, I fear, temporarily indisposed. In what I am about to do, I prefer that there should be no witnesses. You see, Benedict, I have decided that this world has been compelled to harbor you too long."

The voice, so chilling in its complete detachment, started a shiver of cold fear crawling up Sir Gideon's spine. He was compelled to remind himself that he still held the whip hand.

"Fine words, Mandersely," he sneered, "but I believe you'll be forced to swallow them. Kill me and you will never see your precious Lucia Mannering again!" He leaned back in his chair with an air of triumph. "You may believe her to be at Culliford Cross, but I assure you she is not!"

"I know she is not!" Hugo was standing now, rolling up his sleeves in a businesslike fashion. "Come along man, stir yourself!" he snapped suddenly. "Or do you wish me to run you through where you sit?"

Sir Gideon's scalp was prickling. He had the oddest sensation that, in some unbelievable way, everything was slipping from his grasp. But he couldn't lose! Not this time! "What do you mean—you now?"

Hugo stood over him. "I have removed Lucia from that stinking hell where you had the unpardonable callousness to lodge her. She is now at home in her own bed." For the first time the hooded eyes opened wide to betray the full extent of his fury. "Before you die, Benedict, you are going to sweat blood for every second of misery and despair you caused that girl!"

The last vestige of control gone, Sir Gideon

sprang to his feet, his chair crashing to the floor. "Damn you to hell, Mandersely!" he snarled, stripping off coat and boots. "I will have no more of your meddling!"

He stood at last in stocking feet, a bulky, dangerous figure stripped down to shirt and breeches. Hugo indicated the weapons. Sir Gideon seized the nearest sword and stepped back, flexing the blade, testing its balance with a few experimental slashes as he waited for Hugo to push a chair back against the wall.

With only the briefest of salutes, the blades crashed together. From the very outset Sir Gideon, in a white heat of fury, tried to use all his considerable weight in an attempt to force Hugo backward, almost breaking through his guard time and again.

But Hugo, his wrist strong and supple, countered with a kind of daring brilliance. Benedict lunged dangerously; Hugo parried and only partially succeeded in deflecting the blade. The point skidded up his arm, ripping his sleeve to the shoulder and opening up an ugly gash.

"I'll see you in hell yet, my lord!"

"A mere scratch!" Hugo ground out through shut teeth. "You'll need to do better than that!"

Sir Gideon grinned savagely. "I have hardly begun!" He leaped in to finish his work, but Hugo was not to be caught a second time. He parried swiftly and began to press forward his own attack, using all his dexterity of wrist. He lacked the other man's power, but he had been well taught and kept a cool ead. Their stocking feet thudded on the boards; heir breath came quick and heavy.

Benedict was beginning to show signs of tiredness. He repeatedly tried to pierce Hugo's defense, but each time his blade was turned aside. Sweat gathered on his brow and rolled down his face in great drops, clogging his eyelids and threatening his vision, yet he dared not risk wiping it away.

Hugo was able to break through his guard almost at will now, and each time he checked his blade quite deliberately at the last second. Relentlessly he drove Sir Gideon around the room until he pinned him finally against the table. He was dimly aware of hearing sobs as hilt grated against hilt; of the gasping cry: "For God's sake, Mandersely—finish it!" And then his blade was free and plunging home.

The rapier spun from Sir Gideon's grasp, and with a long-drawn sigh he fell, a stain slowly spreading across his shirt front.

Hugo swayed above him, drawing deep, steadying breaths. His vision cleared; his sword hand was clammy and shaking. For the first time he became aware that his own wound was throbbing painfully. Blood had saturated the sleeve and was trickling down his arm.

He stooped to retrieve the discarded weapon, wiped both blades on Franklyn's lace tablecloth, and sat to put on his boots. Then, with a sigh, he collected the rapiers and his coat and unlocked the door.

Two pairs of eyes turned; Toby half-grinned his relief, and then, seeing the blood, sprang to his feet with a cry. Hugo restrained him briefly.

He walked across to Franklyn, who had uttered a low moan on seeing him and thereafter seemed to shrink visibly. The point of Hugo's blade rested lightly against his quivering Adam's apple.

"I don't know how deeply you were implicated in Benedict's foul plotting, Franklyn. If I believed you to be more than just a feckless hanger-on, I would slit your throat here and now."

The terrified eyes bulged.

"However," Hugo's inexorable voice continued, "I am prepared to accord you the benefit of any doubt."

He lowered the pricking rapier point at last. "I leave you to dispose of your late ... friend. I care not how you do it, as long as it doesn't involve me. And then, my friend, you will leave town for good! If you are still here in twenty-four hours, you will be very sorry!"

With Toby at his side, the marquis looked his last on the sweating, quivering travesty of a man who had been responsible for loosing so much misery.

Then he turned contemptuously on his heel.

◆ Chapter 16 ◆

At a little after noon two days later, Hugo arrived in Portland Place clad in a fine mulberry traveling coat and gleaming top boots, his arm in an elegant sling.

His aunt lay half-dozing on a sofa, and straightened up with a little shriek at the sight of her nephew, hastily smoothing down her pink-striped jaconet wrapper and setting straight her cap.

"Lordy, Hugo!" I never expected to see you about so soon! Surely it cannot be right for you to be on your feet?"

"My dear aunt," Hugo drawled with all his old insouciance. "I am not so poor-spirited as to be kept abed by a mere scratch!"

"Then you are to be congratulated!" snapped that good lady. "For my part, I am still far from well. I declare that whole horrid business aged me by ten years at the very least! Were it not for poor Lucia, I should be in my bed."

"Lucia is not worse?"

"No, no, of course she is not!" she said hastily, seeing the alarm spring to his eyes. "In fact, she sleeps a great deal, which Dr. Gordon thinks a good

229

thing. But she has scarcely spoken two words, though we have all tried!"

"Do you think I might see her, aunt?"

"Of course, my boy. Though whether she will be awake . . . ?"

"You see, I am obliged to leave town somewhat urgently. It is Great-Uncle Bertram—"

"Again!" cut in his aunt, incensed. "Must you? Can you not send a message saying that you are unwell? He has no right to use you so abominably!"

Hugo's sleepy eyes lifted a little in amusement. "My dear aunt, I cannot believe him so boorish as to die in order to be disobliging!"

"What! Is he really going this time?"

"So I am led to believe," said Hugo dryly. "And as his heir I am bound to be there, if he so wishes."

They had reached Lucia's room, and Aunt Aurelia scratched gently on the door panel. Chloe came at once.

"Lord Mandersely is come to see your mistress, child. Is she awake?"

Chloe blushed, meeting his lordship's gaze; the bruise on her jaw reminded her vividly of their last meeting.

"She is asleep, m'lady . . . m'lord. Shall I wake her?"

"No!" Hugo spat the word out curtly. He walked to the foot of the bed and stood looking down, treasuring himself the dear face so pale and still against the pillows, deep purple smudges standing out beneath the sweep of her silken lashes.

"Look after her, Aunt," he said abruptly.

When the door had closed, the figure in the bed stirred and two large tears rolled down onto the pillow.

The following morning Dr. Gordon found Lucia up and sitting in a chair by the window.

"Well!" he boomed. "This is a pleasant surprise!"

Without any preamble she announced in a tight voice, "Dr. Gordon, I want to go home, to my grandfather."

He looked at her keenly. "Do you, now? Well, there's no great surprise in that." He lowered his ample proportions into the chair beside her and took her hand in his, patting it gently. "But will you not bide a wee while longer, lassie? You'll not quite be up to the journey yet, I'm thinking."

He felt her fingers tense. "I want to go *now*—as soon as possible. Truly I am not trying to be difficult. *I just have to go right away!*"

She couldn't explain, even to him, that she still felt tainted, that she needed to try to get the smell of that awful place out of her system! She knew that Sir Gideon was dead, that Hugo had killed him. Hetty had been full of it and she had listened, still in a haze of unreality.

Hugo had seen her in that place, and now he had gone away; someone had told her why, but it wasn't important. She must go now herself, before he came back. She couldn't face him, not yet.

Perhaps Dr. Gordon understood better than she thought, for he gave her hand a final pat and said casually, "Aye, well, maybe it would be for the best.

A complete change of scene and some good countr
air will set you up quicker than anything."

He heaved himself out of the chair. "Would yo
like me to broach the matter to Lady Springhope?"

"Would you? I should hate her to be offended. Sh
has been so very kind."

"Leave the good lady to me!" He gave her a con
spiratorial wink, and Lucia stretched a hand to hin
impulsively.

"Thank you," she whispered. "For . . . being so un
derstanding!"

"Ooh, that's what I'm here for, lassie! And mind
now I shall expect to see you returning in a few
weeks' time with the roses blooming again in thos
pretty cheeks!"

It was a day of mellow autumn sunshine wher
Aunt Addie, glancing through the parlor window
saw the dashing yellow curricle drawn by four glossy
chestnut horses being brought nicely to a halt at the
front steps. A funny little man climbed down and
ran to their heads, and Lord Mandersely stepped
down and mounted to the door. She met him in a
flurry of twittering confusion.

He endeavored to put her at ease, and assured her
that he had not informed them of his coming, as he
had no wish to put anyone out.

When, however, he asked how her niece did, she
became even more like an agitated hen, bemoaning
the poor dear child's changed state.

Hugo's heart took a dive. "Changed? How changed?

After ten days I had hoped to find her much improved."

"She is well enough in herself, to be sure ... but so quiet! You know how gay and forthright she was. I ... well, that is, Papa never did tell me what happened in London ... but I have a great fear ... it may have had some permanent effect ..." Aunt Addie pressed a handkerchief to her trembling mouth.

Hugo, by now thoroughly alarmed, demanded curtly to see Colonel Mannering. She scurried ahead of him, sniffing in such a depressing way that it took considerable restraint on Hugo's part to refrain from snapping at her.

On the threshold of the colonel's room, he insisted brusquely that she should say nothing of his visit to her niece, and received an incoherent assent.

The old gentleman rose stiffly from his chair and stood leaning on the ebony cane. "Well, my boy, so you've come at last!"

Hugo acknowledged this forthright greeting and likewise came straight to the point. "What the devil is all this I have been hearing about Lucia, sir?"

Colonel Mannering snorted. "Pshaw! You've been listening to Addie's ravings; never knew a woman with such a morbid turn of mind! What's she been telling you? That Lucy's lost her reason?"

"Something of the sort. It can't be true!"

"Of course it isn't true; a pack of tarradiddle!" Relief flooded Hugo's face. "Mind you, she's not herself, but if you can't remedy that, you're not the man I take you for."

"I hope you may be right."

"I am. But if you'll pardon my saying so, I can't commend your strategy, lad! Leaving the child just when she most needed you!"

"That was unforeseen. But I fear Great-Uncle Bertram remained awkward to the last."

"Gone, has he? Ah well ... poor old Bertram! He had ever a rotten sense of timing. I well remember ..." The colonel became aware of Hugo's look of glazed politeness and said with a twinkle, "But you'll not be wanting to listen to me boring on, eh?"

"At any other time, sir, I should be delighted ..."

"But at this moment you are wishing me at Jericho. Very proper!"

"You know I intend to marry Lucia, sir. You have no objection?"

"Would it make any difference?"

Hugo grinned suddenly. "None whatever, sir."

"Well, you'd best get on with it, then; I can't imagine why it's taken you so long!" The colonel cleared his throat noisily. "By the way, my dear boy ... I don't find it easy to talk about even now, but it must be said! I am forever in your debt with regard to all you did for my little Lucy. When I think what might have happened ..."

"Don't, I beg of you, distress yourself, sir! It is finished, thank God!" The two men gripped hands.

Lucia was in the music room sitting at the pianoforte. She didn't hear the door, and he was able to watch her unseen; drinking in her beauty like a man with a great thirst. She was wearing a simple white gown, and her lovely hair was loosely tied back with

234

a white ribbon. Her slight figure dropped despondently over the keys.

He said deeply, "Good afternoon, Lucia."

She stared violently, her fingers jarring on a tuneless chord, the color coming and going in her face. After a fleeting glance she stood up and moved away toward the window.

"I . . . I didn't know you were here, my lord!"

"Did I frighten you? I'm sorry." He explained why it had taken him so long to come, and she listened politely.

When he had finished, she said, "I am sorry about your great-uncle. So you are now the duke of Troon?"

"I'm afraid so. Shall you mind?"

"No . . . why should I?" That distant politeness was like a wall. For the first time in his life he felt terribly unsure.

"Come and let me look at you!" he commanded.

For a brief moment she stood poised as though for flight, and then she came and stood submissively before him, hoping that he would not hear her heart hammering with the joy and pain of being near him. She had not realized how much she had longed for a sight of that dear, arrogant face.

Hugo put a finger beneath her chin and examined her face minutely, while she stood with eyes cast down. She looked cool and unmoved, but there was a little telltale pulse beating in her throat.

"I had hoped to see you looking better."

She shifted uncomfortably. "And you? Is your arm

recovered? I . . . This is the first chance I have had to thank you . . ."

"I don't want thanks!" said Hugo intensely. "I just want you well and happy again."

"I am quite better now, truly." She slid from under his hand and returned to the window.

God, this is awful! thought Hugo. We aren't getting anywhere.

"How is Toby?"

"You know Toby—and already talking of returning to his regiment."

"Hasn't he done enough?" she murmured bitterly.

"Oh, he is convinced that the worst is over and that the army is going to win out! He could be right at that! But I am not here to talk about Toby. . . ."

Her shoulders had drooped again, and he suddenly found himself saying calmly, "You will see him for yourself very soon, for I am come to take you back to town."

"No!"

His eyebrow lifted. "You can't hide down here forever, you know. What of Hetty? There is very little time left now before the wedding."

"I won't let Hetty down." Lucia's fingers drummed nervously on the window ledge. "I don't need to come to town for that; I can travel to Mandersely from here."

"My aunt is missing you. She has a big party to arrange shortly, and you are so much better at organizing matters than Hetty."

The fingers drummed louder. "They will manage. I . . . don't wish to return."

"I am not interested in what you wish," he said softly. "You are coming back to town with me today."

Slowly she turned, and the old defiant tilt of the chin was back. "Because I am your property and must do as you say? Oh no, sir! Not anymore! I shall speak to Grandpapa—he will not permit it!"

Hugo felt excitement welling up inside him. He almost swept her into his arms there and then, but there was a strong nostalgic urge to play out the game to the end. He said coolly, "I have already spoken to the colonel and have his full permission."

Lucia stared. "I don't believe it! Oh, how despicable to go behind my back!" She stamped her foot. "Since you are a duke you are become more arrogant than ever! Well, *I* shall see him myself and tell him that I do not wish to go with you. I cannot imagine what is so important about this party of Lady Springhope's that it cannot be managed without me!"

"Oh! Did I not tell you?" Hugo's eyes were alight with gentle laughter, but she was too full of angry tears to see. "It is an engagement party. You see, I too am to be married!"

"Oh!" Lucia bit hard on her lip. It was what she had been expecting, but it hurt. "No!" she cried angrily. I will not help with your stupid party! And I am glad you are marrying your countess. I wish you joy of her, for I think you deserve each other!"

She ran headlong for the door, but Hugo was there before her and gathered her into his arms, a struggling, sobbing wild thing.

"Hush now! Not Sophia! Oh, my dearest one ... never Sophia! That was cruel of me! Forgive me!" Holding her with one arm, he tenderly wiped away her tears as they continued to fall. "I just couldn't stand that frozen-faced stranger a moment longer—I wanted my own dear Lucy back. I haven't had a good fight since she went away from me! Oh, come now, little love, be still!"

She was staring at him as though he had taken leave of his senses, and the laughter died from his eyes as he bent his head to kiss her, very gently at first, and then, as with an incoherent cry her struggles ceased and her arms crept up around his neck, he uttered a groan and pulled her closer, crushing the breath from her body as his mouth closed on hers.

When at last he released her, she was rosy and ecstatic and bemused. "It was me!" she gasped. "All the time it was me?"

He gazed down at her in a highly satisfied manner. "From the very first ... it just took a little while to realize it."

"But you never said! Only once I thought ..."

"When Toby was ill? Yes, I was on the point of telling you, but then I mistakenly imagined that you two had changed your minds about each other, and so I kept quiet"—his voice grated suddenly—"and almost lost you!"

"Don't!" She shuddered. "I can't think about that, even now! And I was so sure you were going to marry Sophia. What fools we both were! Oh!" A hand flew to her mouth. "I've just thought—I shall be a duchess!"

Hugo smiled lazily down at her. "Will you like that?"

"I'm not sure." She stepped away from him. "We shall have to be very dignified and not quarrel anymore."

"Impossible!"

"But we must!" she decided with mock seriousness. "Dignity—that's the thing. I shall address you as 'my lord duke'!"

"Lucia!" Hugo advanced upon her threateningly, and she danced away. "You will call me by my right name. For far too long I have put up with 'my lord'—I have no intention of tolerating 'my lord duke' for even a moment. Is that quite clear?"

Head on one side, Lucia appeared to be giving this ultimatum her full consideration. At last she smiled.

"Quite clear, my lord duke," she said demurely.